HALF PAST
nun

Other Sister Mary Teresa mysteries by Monica Quill

A SISTER MARY TERESA MYSTERY

HALF PAST
nun

Monica Quill

St. Martin's Press
New York

HALF PAST NUN. Copyright © 1997 by Monica Quill. All rights reserved. Printed in the United States of America. No part of this book may be used or reproduced in any manner whatsoever without written permission except in the case of brief quotations embodied in critical articles or reviews. For information, address St. Martin's Press, 175 Fifth Avenue, New York, N.Y. 10010.

Library of Congress Cataloging-in-Publication Data

Quill, Monica.
    Half past nun : a Sister Mary Teresa mystery / by Monica Quill.—1st ed.
       p. cm.
    ISBN 0-312-15541-7
    1. Mary Teresa, Sister (Fictitious character)—Fiction. I. Title.
PS3563.A31166H35   1997
813'.54—dc21   97-1182
                                                CIP

First Edition: July 1997

10 9 8 7 6 5 4 3 2 1

HALF PAST
nun

Richard came by the house on Walton Street in the late afternoon and surprisingly accepted when Sister Mary Teresa Dempsey asked him to stay for supper.

"Isn't Lois expecting you at home?" Kim asked. Thus far she had been proud of him. Richard had asked for a soft drink, to her relief. As far as she knew, her brother was a moderate drinker, but there had been enough trouble with alcohol in the family for her to be wary.

"I'll give her a call."

"Good," Emtee Dempsey said, sounding a little surprised herself. She had been plying him with questions about the Chicago police department and was pleased by the prospect of continuing it over the dinner table even though, like Kim, she did not like to keep Richard from his family.

"I'm giving a talk out in Schaumburg later," Richard explained.

"A talk!"

Richard's brows lifted at his sister's reaction. "That's right."

"About what?"

"About this funny business in the suburbs."

"Funny," Joyce cried. "You call murders funny?"

"Not when we can't solve them."

He apparently meant it about giving a talk. That is what he told Lois, using the phone in the kitchen while Kim lent Joyce a hand. The two nuns did not eavesdrop, of course, but they were aware of the uxorious tone Richard's voice had assumed when Lois came on the line.

When Kim had decided to enter the Order of Martha and Mary she never would have dreamt that she and Joyce and Emtee Dempsey would end up in this beautiful house on Walton Street in Chicago, the gift of an alumna, designed by Frank Lloyd Wright. The college had been closed and sold, most members of the Order had drifted away, returning to the world, in the phrase, casualties of changes introduced too swiftly to be absorbed. Through the turmoil, Sister Mary Teresa had remained firm as a rock and Kim and Joyce had attached themselves to her. The old nun still wore the traditional habit, but tolerated the modern dress of Kim and Joyce.

At the table, Richard glanced at his watch several times and Kim asked him how long it would take to drive to Schaumburg.

"That depends. This time of night, it should be a straight shot."

The subject of his talk was the subject of his conversation with Emtee Dempsey. Over the past months, the bodies of three young women had been found and were thought to be the victims of the same killer. Two other young women were reported missing and it was feared they might be added to the list. Richard had been put in charge of the team working on the case.

"Doesn't Schaumburg have its own police?"

"There are several jurisdictions involved. That's why we have the team, to coordinate efforts. Two of the bodies were found in Schaumburg, the third outside of Elgin."

"Which has its own police."

"Sister, there are a hundred and twenty-six police jurisdictions in the greater Chicago area."

"Isn't that a bit redundant?"

"Would you like to persuade a township or county it no longer needs police of its own?"

"I see what you mean."

"I'm not sure centralization would be an improvement. Being linked by computer is one thing, but to have one jurisdiction?" Richard shook his head.

"That was the genius of the Empire. Centralization but keeping as much of the existing local order as possible."

"The Empire?" Richard said, a fatal mistake. The old nun was soon embarked on a lecture dealing with the way in which Rome had spread its tentacles in all directions, across the Mediterranean, to the east and to the west, reaching ultimately the point where the wall was built across Britain to keep the untamable Scots at bay. She was about to illustrate a point by bringing in Evelyn Waugh's novel *Helena* when Joyce returned from the kitchen and intervened.

"You are approaching the best time from Schaumburg to the Loop, according to the WBBM traffic reporter."

Richard pushed back from the table unceremoniously, thanked his hostess and the cook, and headed for the door. Kim went along to let him out.

"Drive carefully," she said, kissing him on the cheek.

"Hey, I can get nagged at home."

"How is home?"

"The kids would love to see you. It's been a while."

"I know."

"I'll have Lois call."

"Have her include Joyce."

"Joyce is who we want. You're the excuse."

Watching him bound down the steps and across the walk to where his unmarked car was parked where it shouldn't have been, Kim felt a rush of affection for her brother. Richard and Lois and their children were all she had now by way of family—not counting all the cousins and half cousins and other semi-strangers who showed up at wakes and weddings.

"Why does Schaumburg ring a bell?" Sister Mary Teresa asked when Kim rejoined them.

Joyce made a face. "I think of it as more of a hum. A hum with a little thud at the end."

"It's where Joanne works."

"Joanne, Joanne."

"Library, visiting author, interview," Kim prompted and caused a cold eye of remembrance to be turned on her. "I only said you'd think about it."

Joanne, a librarian, was an alumna of the college of the Sisters of Martha and Mary, which had thrived west of the city until the renewals that followed Vatican II decimated their ranks and all but destroyed the order. The school had been sold off and the money spent—in darker moods Emtee Dempsey said squandered—in various ways. But thanks to the help of some stalwart lay members of the board, Benjamin Rush and Katherine Senski, this house on Walton Street, not far from the Newberry Library, as well as a lake property in Michigan, had been shored against their ruin. Emtee Dempsey, Kim, and Joyce were the three remaining members of a once flourishing community, and they recently had been joined by a postulant, Margaret Mary Horan, who was widowed several years ago and who was now considering entering the order. She had been an undergraduate with Kim and brought welcome talents to their little community. She knew all about computers. Emtee Dempsey had been doubtful about admitting Margaret Mary—"We want youth, sisters, youth!"—and unimpressed by the computer expertise. But then she herself wrote with an old-fashioned fountain pen and probably considered it a dangerous innovation as she worked away on her history of the twelfth century. Moreover, she always insisted that Margaret Mary be at her side.

Margaret Mary asked, "What is it that Sister Mary Teresa was going to think about?"

"Have you ever heard of Cecilia Vespertina?" the old nun asked.

Margaret Mary thought for a moment and then, looking disappointed in herself, said, "I suppose it's someone I should know."

"It is not. If the name were familiar to you I might regard it as a sign you have no vocation." Emtee Dempsey was superior of the house and now acted in the role of novice mistress as well. "Sister Kimberly, you had best describe this person. My account might appear less objective."

Kimberly gave a sketch of the author Joanne had booked to lecture at the Schaumburg library. Cecilia Vespertina—Joanne had checked and still insisted this was the woman's legal name, not a pen name—was the very successful author of what are called self-help books. Dr. Vespertina was soon to be a speaker at the Schaumburg library. She belonged to the school holding that the cardinal principle of mental health is, in effect, to fall in love with yourself. The reader was urged to cease being judgmental with herself and to discard standards and criteria emanating from who knew where and thanks to which one was always falling short and feeling bad. Feeling bad was bad and Cecilia would have none of it. She wrote with an Olympian omniscience, offered advice with a Kantian confidence, and had modified the Principle of Utility to read: That action is best which is for the greatest good of number one.

"I am borrowing from Sister Mary Teresa's less objective account," Kim explained.

"This person," the old nun said. "This person who has managed to find some minor therapeutic value in religious

5

belief, so long as it does not induce guilt or suggest in any way that one is a sinner, wishes to interview what she is pleased to call a 'typical' nun to see what psychological effect incarceration in the cloister has had."

"Oh, Sister, that isn't fair. She wants to interview someone who has been in the religious life for some years."

"I know the breed, Sister Kimberly. She wants to peer at a specimen she has already classified in advance."

"Joanne thinks it is more. She finds in her last book signs of an opening toward religious faith."

"Please." Sister Mary Teresa was trying to stop her ears but since she wore the massive starched traditional headdress of the order, which had been likened to a wounded seagull about to land, this was a difficult maneuver. "That dreadful, dreadful jargon. For years I had to tolerate slurs on the accurate and precise language of the Scholastics and now to hear this drivel parading as significant speech is more than mortal man can bear."

"You use the term inclusively of course," Kim teased.

"Exactly." Emtee Dempsey chose to regard Kim's remark as adding to her argument.

Kim noticed that Margaret Mary both appreciated the humor and the underlying serious points in such diatribes. No one who failed to see what a privilege it was to live with Sister Mary Teresa, who was a living link with the order as it once gloriously had been and as they hoped to see it restored, would be approved by Kim and Joyce for entry into the order.

"Richard is speaking under the auspices of Joanne's library too, Sister," Kim told their newest member. "There's been all kinds of publicity. Lieutenant Richard Moriarity on Chicago's Latest Serial Killer."

"Tell Sister the librarian joke, Kim."

"I will not."

"She'd love it. So would Margaret Mary."

"Joyce, you are a troublemaker."

"Tell me," Emtee Dempsey commanded. "Joyce will give us no peace until you do."

Kim sighed. "Remember, I am simply reporting this. You know what they call journals and magazines and periodicals generally in libraries?"

"Oh no," Emtee Dempsey said. "No."

"You asked for it."

Joyce said to Margaret Mary, "They call them serials."

"A serial killer," Kim recited, "is someone who discontinues subscriptions to magazines."

There was general moaning and groaning all around, with the old nun again making another effort to stop her ears. Joyce offered an alternative: the serial killer as someone who devours Wheaties.

"Get it?" she asked. "Get it?"

"You're going to get it if you don't watch out," the old nun said, heaving herself to her feet and bowing her head. Silence fell and then they all said the grace after meals.

2

The facilities of the Schaumburg library rivaled those of many college libraries. The building was spanking new, functional, and in every department—the number of departments astounded Richard—the last word was the rule: in adult books, children books, video, audio, and in databases such that sophisticated research could be done. It was teeming with people, only a fraction of whom were there for Richard's talk.

"We're the envy of the area," Joanne replied to his comments. "Whatever we want we get."

She was a small woman of swift movements, suggesting one of those shorebirds with long legs who scamper along beaches. Her clothes seemed particularly flamboyant because they covered so small a body—a flaming yellow suit, with a scarf of black polk dots, and stiletto heels on her platform shoes. Her hair was of indecisive hue, indicating that last week's shade might have been altogether different.

"We have a huge tax base," she explained. "That is the bright side of Schaumburg's blight."

The suburb did rise up as a city of its own, tall, glistening buildings, malls, office complexes. Richard had heard it referred to as the antithesis of city planning, but the thing itself had its attractions. Posters advertising his talk were everywhere, softening any negative feelings he might have been inclined to have.

Joanne took him to a room where Hirtz, the local chief, and representatives from other departments in the collar counties awaited. Richard recognized Schwartz of Niles and Cy Horvath of Fox River. They shook hands like lodge brothers, and then they were all off to the auditorium.

"Did I ask if it's okay if we tape your talk?" Joanne asked.

"What's my royalty?"

"Oh, it's not for commercial use."

"I'm kidding, I'm kidding." The honorarium he had been offered had been so generous Lois was unsure how she would use it. "I'll give you the text for the archives," he said.

Humor, it was clear, was wasted on Joanne. Or she had a demanding taste. But then, Richard reflected, I'm a cop here to talk about three grisly killings that we think may be the work of the same man. He could hardly be expected to be treated as a stand-up comic.

The auditorium was jammed. A murmur greeted the appearance of the phalanx of policeman. Joanne led them to the platform and arrayed them on chairs; she then stepped to the podium and peered over it, throwing her words up at the mike. During her flowery introduction, Hirtz leaned toward Richard and asked if he could get his autograph. But the little librarian got quickly to the business at hand. It was clear the place was full because of the fear people felt that another monster was loose in the Chicago area. Richard's role was to let them know that the police forces of the city and suburbs shared their concern and were doing something about it. When he took his place behind the podium and looked over the applauding crowd he was resolved to give it to them straight.

He began with a brief history of the serial killer—Jack

the Ripper, the Boston Strangler, Ted Bundy, John Wayne Gacy—and the way in which police procedures had adapted only gradually to the phenomena. Two things had made the difference, cooperation between jurisdictions and computers, and they were two sides of the same coin.

"For purposes of this investigation, all the police departments in the greater Chicago area—municipal, township, county, large and small—are working as a single department."

The great difficulty with such a killer was the lack of a link between motive and victim. The victim could be anyone—a male of course for the homosexual serial killer, a female for the heterosexual—but apart from sex and attractiveness there seemed to be no other requirements.

"The killings are random and they are impulsive, spur-of-the-moment deeds. We rely almost exclusively on physical evidence and the psychological pattern that has emerged from the study of such killers."

As he spoke of the three victims, he remembered how terribly difficult it was for the families to accept that their daughters just happened to become victims. It was highly unlikely that the killer even knew who they were or had been stalking them for long. They could so easily not have been victims. Going to one's car in a mall parking lot in the late afternoon, while it was still light out, does not sound like a risky thing to do. But for one of the girls, Irma Walsh, it had meant death. Another, Amy Kuharic, apparently had stopped to talk to someone in a parked car, also during the day. Her backpack and gloves had been found on the street.

"Maybe the driver pretended to be lost and asked directions, opening the passenger door to do so. The victim approached, she was grabbed, pulled into the car struggling, and was never seen alive again."

Where and when the third victim, Elizabeth Webster,

had been taken was unknown, but Richard's message was that it could have been anytime, anywhere.

He was not there to alarm his audience but neither did he want to offer empty reassurance. A team of highly capable investigators was at work, but it was likely that it would take a long time; they could not say there would not be other victims. Because of the nature of the case, they expected more victims. But eventually they would get the killer. There was complete conviction in his voice because he was confident he was right: They would run this killer to ground.

The applause had a different feel than before the talk, although it would have been difficult to say what the difference was. Richard wanted to think that the audience knew he had leveled with them. And now he would take their questions.

The first questioner wanted to know how long Richard thought it would take some wacko judge to release the killer after he was convicted. Richard tossed that one back. Was the questioner sure some lawyer couldn't convince a jury that the killer was the real victim? For the most part, the questions were good ones.

"You referred to the killer several time as a man," a lady asked. "Do you know this or is this a guess?"

"I was using the word in the inclusive sense," Richard said. "I suppose I might have said person. Or perdaughter."

Dangerous waters these, and he rowed away from them. Fortunately that line was not pursued.

"Didn't anyone hear them scream, didn't anyone notice?"

That was what investigators were in the process of finding out by interviewing everyone they could find who was in the area at the time each victim was kidnapped.

The discussion turned to preventive measures that might be taken, and Richard called his colleagues to the podium to add to what he had to say. Hirtz was a great proponent of mace, Schwartz warned against jogging or walking alone at any time of the day. "Go by twos," Horvath said. "Like nuns used to."

The formal session was called to an end and people swarmed the platform, a mixed blessing when someone wanted to attach himself to an investigator and let them know how much they knew about police work. A particularly intense young man asked Richard what he thought the ordinary citizen should do.

"We covered that a bit in the question period, didn't we?"

"In generalities, yes."

"What did you have in mind?"

"Forming groups like the Guardian Angels."

Vigilante groups are the bane of police work, so Richard took the time to dissuade this fellow from that sort of thinking. When he turned away from him he faced an attractive woman whose yellow blond hair was braided and pulled around her neck to lie across her bosom. She smiled into Richard's face, fixing him with her wide blue eyes.

"You were wonderful," she said.

"Thank you."

"This would make a wonderful book, do you realize that?"

"I'm not a writer."

"I am. I want to explore the possibility with you."

"You're a writer?"

"Yes." She kept her eyes fixed on him while she opened her purse. "Here is my card. Do you have a card?"

"Look, I don't have time to write a book."

"You had time to give this talk. I taped it, by the way." She pulled a recorder halfway from her purse, then dropped it in again. "A few more sessions like this, with you just talking, and I'd have enough to start on."

"That sounds pretty easy."

"For you." She smiled. "Not for me. Of course it would be your book."

Richard was flattered, of course, and weakened by the fact that she was an extraordinarily attractive woman. She made him think of the illustration on the cover of *Kristin Lavransdatter*, Lois's favorite novel, when he looked at her. It seemed the path of least resistance to give her his card.

"Good," she said. "I'll call."

"What's your name?"

Ice broke, snow melted, the fjords flowed when she smiled. "It's on my card. Astrid Johansen."

"A good Irish name?"

She flourished his card. "A good Norwegian name."

On the long drive back he thought of many aspects of the lecture. He had been surprised how easy it was, but all he had done was talk about what he did, what he knew. The applause could be addictive, he saw that. But it was Astrid Johansen's suggestion that he write a book about his police experiences that had made the deepest impression. Lois would like that. His colleagues would resent it and subject him to much ribbing. But what if the book was successful? He imagined it on the bestseller list, author tours, giving the speech he had given tonight to fascinated readers across the nation. And he thought how much fun it would be to show up on Walton Street if he were an author, like the venerable Sister Mary Teresa Dempsey.

3

Joanne called the house on Walton Street the following morning to report on Richard's success in Schaumburg the night before.

"He scared us all out of our wits, of course, but I think that's for the best. We've become so complacent in the suburbs, thinking all the violence is back there in the city."

Kim took the call in her room, where she was emulating Emtee Dempsey by writing a given number of pages every day. Her role as research assistant to the old nun, however demanding it became, was not to exonerate her from her task as a graduate student in history at Northwestern. Resolution was one thing, execution another, however, and it was not wholly unfair of Kim to blame her lack of progress on Emtee Dempsey. But then, she learned more working with the old nun anyway, and she wasn't in a hurry. She was where she intended to be for the foreseeable future. Taking such calls as Joanne's was a sure way to get off schedule, but Joyce was shopping and it went without saying that the old nun did not answer the phone.

"Of course you know I have an ulterior motive for calling, Sister," said Joanne, referring to the question of Cecilia Vespertina.

"I haven't made any progress, I'm afraid."

"But she hasn't definitely refused?"

"No, but please don't take that as encouragement. To be honest, she enjoys having the invitation to complain about."

"I can absolutely assure her it will be a minimum of bother."

"She won't be coming to the lecture, Joanne."

"Oh, that was Dr. Vespertina's idea, not mine. And she was thinking generally, not in terms of Sister Mary Teresa Dempsey. If she's going to meet an older nun I can't think of a better one for her to interview, can you?"

"Certainly not."

"Would it help if I spoke to Sister?"

"I don't think so. Not at the moment, certainly, she is incommunicado in her sanctum sanctorum."

"Have her say a prayer for me."

Kim smiled at the phone after she hung up. Obviously, referring to the old nun's study in her own baroque fashion invited misunderstanding. The three of them had been up at the crack of dawn for Mass in their chapel here in the house, the cardinal having assigned them a retired monsignor, Anselm McCarthy, to say Mass for them in the morning. He was scarcely taller than Emtee Dempsey, had a face almost as red as his monsignorial sash, and was delighted to celebrate in the *Novus Ordo*—Latin, but with the liturgical changes of recent years. Monsignor McCarthy had been disappointed to learn that there were no chaplain quarters in the house.

"It was not designed as a convent, Monsignor. We just make do with the house as it is."

Emtee Dempsey had made it sound as if they were camping out. Hardly a week went by when they did not receive an offer for the house, conveyed apologetically by realtors who knew they would never sell. Sometimes, Kim regretted that the house was so historic—Wright-designed homes were rare and sought after—but then it would not have been as nice a house otherwise.

In any case, they had spent their time in chapel, had their breakfast, and were well into their day when Joanne had called asking for a prayer. Perhaps she imagined Emtee Dempsey drifting in and out of chapel all day long, breathing prayers for far-flung alumnae.

Kim felt duplicitous with Joanne on the Cecilia Vespertina matter. If it had been her decision, she would have given a flat no and that would have been it. But the old nun saw such possibilities of pungent commentary in the work and attitude of the self-help author that she simply could not put it away.

"The woman is so incredible on the page, one is bound to wonder what she is like in person," said Emtee Dempsey.

"Joanne says she is very pleasant on the phone, but demanding. She is on what seems to be a triumphal tour and she is used to being feted and fawned over, or so Joanne leads me to think."

"But she put it differently?"

"I'm not quoting her verbatim, no."

"Joanne never met her personally?"

"She did send a video based on her book, *Nine Ways to Self-Esteem.*"

"How the Desert Fathers could have profited from reading Dr. Vespertina! Or imagine Catherine of Siena working on her self-esteem."

"Or Blessed Abigail Keineswegs," Kim said loyally, putting in a plug for their foundress.

Katherine Senski, dean of Chicago reporters—she had rejected with contempt the suggestion that she might prefer *deaconess* to *dean*—and veteran ally of Emtee Dempsey in matters concerning the Order of Martha and Mary, soon came to lunch on Walton Street, it being Tuesday and her regular day to join them.

"Of course you must ask her here," Katherine said when the Cecilia Vespertina matter came up. "But on condition that I too be invited. Interview indeed. I'll wager she hasn't the faintest idea what an interview consists of. She doubtless has a bag of loaded questions and a headful of conclusions before she begins."

"Have you read her books?" Kim asked.

"I don't have to read her books. I have paged through similar balderdash from time to time, in the interests of keeping up on the declension of modern society."

"I don't think you can keep up on a declension, Katherine," Sister Mary Teresa said.

"You know what I mean."

"I know you cannot mean what you said."

"You are diverting us from the main subject."

"And who decided that this innocuous writer of harmless self-help books should be our main subject? I had hoped to talk of my morning work."

"Innocuous! Harmless! I have, as it happens, done a little research on the lady. Her name as you will have guessed is acquired. She was born Louise Brighton, the daughter of an American GI and an English mother. The father was killed in the war and it was not until Louise was a teenager that she took advantage of her citizenship and came to the United States. She immediately set up as an expert in matters European, English as well as continental. A British accent combined with the guts of a burglar will take one very far indeed. It took her from a relatively modest position on an Austin, Minnesota, paper to a syndicated column. It was then that she discovered her perverse knack for telling people exactly what they want to hear, recast in all but impenetrable jargon. Her first book was an assembly of articles, but from that point on she has been primarily an author, lecturer, and counselor."

Having delivered herself of this biographical sketch,

Katherine sat back, wound her fingers into the rope of beads hanging round her neck, and looked around the table for reaction.

"Where are on earth did you find all that?"

"In a standard reference book of American authors."

"But wouldn't she have written that herself?"

Katherine let go of her beads and cocked an eye at Sister Mary Teresa. "Of course she would have. And you're right. We would be fools to take it literally. I am glad you made that point."

It was clear nonetheless that Katherine felt deflated. And it did not help her disposition to have Emtee Dempsey speculating that a good portion of the items in that biographical entry would have to be factual.

"I tried to read *Nine Ways to Self-Esteem.*"

"For Lenten reading, I trust."

Joyce said, "Look, I know people who claim to have gotten a lot out of her books. Women at the day care center."

Joyce volunteered four afternoons a week for several hours. It gave her an opportunity to be around children and get involved in less heady conversations than those common in the house.

"Such books sell by the bushel," Katherine agreed. "But so do those big chubby romance novels with the half-dressed heroine on the cover. Wherever I go I see women absorbed in those things. Considering the context, I suppose it could be said that Cecilia Vespertina is no worse than many others."

Kim said, "Somehow I doubt that she would settle for so modest an estimate."

Kim had made a synopsis of *Nine Ways* at Emtee Dempsey's request. The assumptions of the book could be described as extraordinarily optimistic or extraordinarily naive, depending on whether the reader had any awareness of the evil in the world. What possible good could Cecilia Vespertina's incantatory exercises have been for the victims of the serial killer Richard and the others were pursuing? Or to the killer himself? Before the method could be applied, one would have to redesign the universe as well as human beings. Cecilia seemed to think her nine ways would do that. To call the assumption of her work pagan would insult a host of intelligent pagans.

"Give me a summary sentence," Emtee Dempsey had asked, weighing the six-page synopsis Kim gave her.

"Wishing will make it so."

After reading the synopsis and flipping through the book, the old nun agreed. "She should be writing lyrics for romantic songs."

All this was very critical of a woman whom millions regarded as a moral and psychological guide. Her visit to Chicago had been hyped not only by the Schaumburg library, but by the publicity department of Cecilia Vespertina's publisher as well. She would be on all the talk shows, she would sign books in the Loop, but the appearance in Schaumburg was the great event. Kim suspected that Katherine and Emtee Dempsey were as curious to meet the author as she was.

"I'll make arrangements with Joanne," she said.

The old nun sighed. "I suppose."

"Let me get out my schedule book," Katherine said. "I don't want a conflict."

The call to Joanne altered Kim's day. Mitzi Earl, the publisher's designated publicist for its lucrative author, was already in town and said she'd hop in a cab and be there as soon as she could. Kim had little choice but to agree. Besides, the visit confirmed that they had indeed crossed the Rubicon and the much discussed interview would indeed take place.

4

Mitzi Earl had gone to Pepperdine and spent much of her undergraduate years playing volleyball on the beach when she wasn't playing with the varsity team. Her serves hooked and sliced or dropped suddenly, she was the most in-your-face defensive player at the net, she was tall and slim and still bronze as a goddess. She had been hired by the West Coast office of Ethos Books and, when her touch became apparent, was brought east. For a year and a half she had been assigned exclusively to the enlarging and magnifying of the reputation of Cecilia Vespertina.

"It sounds exciting," the surprisingly lovely Sister Kimberly said, after getting Mitzi settled in the little office by the front door. The other nun, Joyce, was bringing iced tea.

"I know," replied Mitzi.

"Isn't it?"

"I feel I've helped create a monster." She had peered down the hall when she came and now she looked around the room. "Is this place really a convent?"

"Yes."

"And you're a nun?"

"That's right. So is Joyce."

The lines left by her smile were etched in Mitzi's tanned

skin and seemed to form a parenthesis around her "Oh." Mitzi managed to conceal her disappointment. Kim and Joyce were dressed pretty much like other young women. Mitzi murmured that she had expected traditional habits.

"Dress blues?" Joyce asked. "Wait until you meet Sister Mary Teresa."

"Tell us about Cecilia," Kim said, after Joyce had poured tea for them all.

"Hey, I'm here to do an advance on the nun she's going to meet."

"I'll introduce you to Sister Mary Teresa after two-thirty."

"Is she praying or something?"

"Napping. She is in her eighth decade."

"Wow."

"Have you read all Cecilia's books?" Joyce asked.

Mitzi looked over both shoulders. "I haven't read any of them. I've heard her so often and after all the meetings we have in public relations, I feel I could write them myself. I've really come to wonder about people since I went to work for Cece. I mean, what she says, and what people hear can be so different. I think that's her real gift. To say something that can be interpreted in dozens of different ways. She gets credit for them all, of course."

"She sounds tough to work for."

Mitzi regretted that she had been so outspoken about their prize author and she added some correctives. Cecilia was a challenge to work for, totally unpredictable, a little spoiled now, but who wouldn't be after the way she's been treated for several years?

"She is moody. Sometimes I think she needs an audience to be herself now. Alone, she is quiet, doesn't talk much. But when she's in front of a group, or when the television camera is on her, she is magnificent."

"What's this interest in nuns?"

Mitzi wrinkled her nose. "The official reason is that she

thinks that in this year of the woman more attention ought to be paid to one of the oldest institutions of western civilization, religious women, nuns."

"What's the unofficial reason?"

Mitzi spoke in a whisper. "She doesn't know I know this. She was raised Catholic."

"There's certainly no trace of it in her work."

"Isn't there? Maybe it's there because it is so absent."

"That's very shrewd."

"I get paid to be shrewd."

"Do you still play volleyball?" Joyce asked.

"I can't! I tore the ligaments in my knee and then tore them again after the operation. I could have been a pro."

Mitzi was predictably knocked over when she met Emtee Dempsey, who rose from behind her desk when they came in, her great headdress lifting too, seeming to be elevating her. She held out her hand.

"So this is Cecilia Vespertina."

"No, no, Sister, This is Mitzi Earl. She works for the publisher that publishes the books we've been talking about."

"But why didn't the author come?"

"That's on Friday, Sister. She's not even in town yet."

When Mitzi's job was explained to the old nun, Emtee Dempsey likened her to John the Baptist, making straight the ways of Cecilia Vespertina.

"You probably think I don't know who John the Baptist was," Mitzi said.

"I think nothing of the sort. You must warn Dr. Vespertina that I will not be condescended to or treated like a relic from another time. People act like this with no intention of being rude, but it is both rude and wrong. I say this not out of a concern for my own feelings. People can treat me as they wish. But if I consent to speak with her about what it is to be a nun, I take on the awesome responsibility of speaking on behalf of a great many women, most of them better equipped than I to perform the task."

Mitzi nodded, but her eyes were constantly drawn to the shelves that covered four walls of the study. "What a wonderful collection of books."

"Are you interested in books?"

"Sister! Mitzi works for a publisher."

They were all so nice, Mitzi thought, after you got over the initial shock that these women actually have taken vows of poverty, chastity, and obedience. The ancient one you could imagine never having been young and figure, so what, what is she giving up, but the young ones brought it home. Mitzi found it hard to believe that something like this was still going on.

That was Cece's angle, of course, only it wasn't that much of a surprise to her that there were such women in the world. She had been taught by nuns, for heaven's sake. Maybe she just wanted to assure herself that all that was still going on, that it was there to fall back on, if it ever came to that.

That was the benign interpretation. What Mitzi feared, and couldn't very well tell these three women—four when you counted the widow who was thinking of joining—was that Cecilia Vespertina planned to do a real number on them. Mitzi had been brought up Unitarian, at least that's the church they went to the three or four times she could remember going. The only people who seemed really marked by their religious upbringing were Jews and Catholics. Apparently there was no way you could stop being a Jew, and the same indelible mark seemed to attach to Catholics. They might stop practicing, complain about how awful it was to be brought up that way, apologize every time the Pope opened his mouth, and suggest that there really wasn't any difference between Catholics and everyone else, but of course no one believed that, including the lapsed Catholics. They couldn't leave it alone. Cece surely didn't practice her religion and most of her memories seemed unhappy. So the women in the house on Walton Street had better get ready. Mitzi felt like the Trojan Horse, welcomed into the house, only to lay it open to the predatory Cecilia.

On the other hand, that little old nun with the wingding of a headdress looked like she could handle herself.

5

ois wanted to hear all about the talk in Schaumburg and Richard gave her a pretty full account. To her he could express how surprised and happy he was at how well it went. But when he mentioned the woman who wanted to help him write a book, the mood changed.

"If you need any help, I'll help you," Lois said.

"Neither one of us has written anything."

"Has she?"

He realized he hadn't asked. She had said she was a writer, but that was a claim anyone could make. All it need mean was that the person hoped someday to publish something.

"For all I know she was joking."

"Then why did you bring it up?"

"I'm sorry I did, okay? Thanks for spoiling my evening."

"Spoil your evening! You're out having a big triumph and I'm dying to hear about it and you're telling me it's all so nice and the next thing you're talking about collaborating with some strange woman on a book."

He took her in his arms, though it took some doing, since she kept squirming away and she was crying now. Why hadn't he insisted that she come along? It would have been great if she had been there and didn't have to get it second hand from him. On the other hand, before the event he had no idea how it would go and if he was going to bomb he sure as hell didn't want Lois there suffering through it with him.

"I promise not to write a book."

"Oh, go ahead. I don't care. Now that you're famous . . . "

"Come on."

"Well you *will* be. You're in the paper every day and that's the way it's going to be until you catch that monster. Can you imagine what it'll be like then?"

"I can imagine what it will be like if we don't catch him soon."

"What's that writer's name?"

"She gave me her card."

"Where is it?"

He had put it in his wallet, but he made a show of looking for it, emptying his pockets, checking the suit he had worn, finally fishing it out of his wallet. Lois took it.

"Astrid Johansen. It doesn't say she's a writer."

"We can look her up and see what's she done."

"One thing about her, she is the first one to see there is a real story here."

"Well, if she calls, I'll talk with her."

She called the next day, asking if he had thought about her suggestion.

"My wife and I talked about it last night, as a matter of fact."

"Does she approve?"

"She figures you must be pretty good to have seen the possibility before anyone else."

They met at Ascoli's in the Loop, which was more of a tavern than a restaurant, a place favored by the press people who covered headquarters. The menu was chalked up, ordering was like bidding at the Merchandise Mart, but somehow everyone got served and conversations were carried on despite the constant din.

"The first thing we need is an agreement. Your wife is right, I'm only the first to see the possibilities in your story. There will be others, believe me. Have you done a check on me?"

He laughed. "I haven't had time. You want the goulash?"

She wanted the goulash, and beer and dark bread. A good thing, since Ascoli's served only one meal. If you didn't like it, you went somewhere else for that day.

"You have to know my credentials." She handed him a vita. Her list of publications filled pages. Mostly articles, but there were three books.

"I see you've never done a collaboration before."

"No. You'll also see I've never done any crime stories, fiction or factual. I don't think that's a drawback. Did you see the movie *Alive!*?"

"The downed airliner in the Andes? Not while I'm eating."

"A modern version of the Donner Party. The man who wrote that had written nothing but novels prior to doing it. Piers Paul Read. There are certain real events that have drama built right into them, but it can be stifled in the telling. You know what it's like when someone who can't tell a story attempts to tell what you also know."

"That's usually me."

She smiled this away. "Already I see tensions and dramatic conflicts that would give structure to the story." She stopped. "I don't want to go very far into what I think we can do together until I know we're going to do it together."

"What kind of a deal do you have in mind?"

"Financially? A straight split of royalties and other income. You get top billing with me as helping you. Or your name could appear alone and you could thank me in the

Introduction. It's all one with me. I want to do this book."

"What do we do, shake hands?"

"I have an agent. He can represent us both, or you could get your own agent. A lawyer would do. What we need first is a written agreement among ourselves, spelling out as many contingencies as we can think up so that there is no room for misunderstanding later. Then we need an agreement with a publisher. My agent thinks he has a good chance with a major publisher who will seal his interest with a sizable advance."

"Advance?"

"Against royalties. Say he gives two hundred thousand dollars. We would get nothing more until the book had earned us two hundred thousand in royalties."

"Is that just a Monopoly Money figure?"

"My agent will ask for more than that."

Richard concentrated on his goulash, not trusting himself to comment on even the remote possibility of getting that kind of money. If she were right about the advance and they split fifty-fifty, he would have one hundred thousand dollars. Of course there would be taxes.

"What are the taxes on that kind of money?"

"That sounds like we have an agreement."

"We do."

"I'll have my agent draw up a statement and you can have it checked by a lawyer. Okay?"

"Okay. How exactly will we do this? You mentioned taping interviews."

She straightened the yellow braid that lay upon her breast. "I've been thinking about it. I think I should be at your side at all times, following the investigation step by step. It will make the account more vivid."

Richard thought about it. He foresaw trouble—with his colleagues, who wouldn't want a civilian hanging around; with the press, who would rightly see favoritism; maybe

28

with his superiors, who would object to him making a profit from work he was paid by the city to do.

"Let me think about it."

"One way or the other I have to know what's going on when it's going on."

"You really are eager to do this story, aren't you?"

"Yes. I deeply resent some madman making me feel unsafe, as if at any moment he might spring out of the dark at me. More and more women are going to feel that way. He has to be stopped. And I guess I want to see what sort of bastard he is when you catch him."

Richard was torn from the pleasures of anticipating the successful completion of his task to the grim task itself by a message from downtown. A young woman had just successfully fended off an effort to abduct her.

"Where is she?"

"The Palmer House."

"The Palmer House?"

"That's where she's staying."

An out-of-town visitor? If the attack on the woman was indeed related to the unknown killer Richard's team had started to refer to as Oscar, the pressure on the team would be increased considerably. The city was dependent on its convention and visitor revenue, and the suggestion that it wasn't safe to walk the streets of Chicago could be devastating.

Two officers, Maggie West and Pat Dougherty, were with the woman, a Mitzi Earl, and the story had not yet broken so he was able to go right up. There were modest single rooms in the Palmer House hotel but this was not one of them. The suite was definitely VIP. Richard's anxiety increased. A famous out-of-towner would complicate things even more.

The young woman was in the bedroom being attended

to by the hotel physician. Maggie came into the sitting room to brief Richard.

"Where's she from?"

Maggie wore a charcoal gray pinstripe suit and salmon pink silk shirt and looked more like a female executive than a cop. "New York."

He looked around the room. "Who is she?"

"She does PR for a publisher."

"What happened?"

"Some guy tried to push her into a car."

"Push her?"

"The back door of this car was standing open as she was coming along the sidewalk. It caught her curiosity and she must have walked closer to it. The next think she knew, she was pushed from behind, grabbed, and maneuvered to-ward the open door."

"How'd she escape?"

Maggie's eyes widened a little. "One hand on the top of the door, the other on the top of the car, she used the momentum of the push to vault over the door."

"Over it?"

"The landing wasn't so good."

"Did she get a look at him?"

Maggie nodded. This would be the first actual sighting of Oscar, if that's who it was. And if this happened on a Loop sidewalk there were other potential witnesses.

"Where did this take place?"

"Walton Street."

"Walton Street!"

"She'd had an appointment up there. It happened moments after she came outside."

"How'd she get back here?"

"She took a cab," Maggie said, and it was clear she thought it was one brave young lady in the next room. But for the moment it was the mention of Walton Street that eclipsed all else for Richard. He went on into the bedroom.

The girl on the bed looked athletic enough to have done what Maggie described, but she had paid the price. One side of her face was pretty banged up and her knees looked like a peon penitent's. The doctor was applying disinfectant to the cuts on her knees.

"That's the one that been operated on twice."

"What for?"

"Torn ligaments." She looked up at Richard as if she recognized him.

"I'm Richard Moriarity, Chicago police."

"Mitzi Earl. Do you have a sister who's a nun?"

He laughed. "As soon as I heard that this happened on Walton Street I was afraid that's where you were."

"You make it sound disreputable."

She might be banged up a little but it was clear this was no hysterical woman. Richard pulled up a chair and told her that they had reason to think that what happened to her was connected with other events in the Chicago area.

"The serial killer?" Mitzi asked.

Richard looked around at Maggie. "How much have you told her?"

But Mitzi said, "I got in yesterday. Reading the papers is part of my job."

"You think that's who it was?"

"I never thought of it until you said what you did."

It had occurred to the house physician, however, and he'd had his secretary put in a discreet call to the police. The hotel management was of course interested in total discretion. A Mr. Foye was now in the sitting room talking with Pat Dougherty.

If it hadn't been for Mitzi's injuries and her manner Richard would have suspected they had an imaginative young woman on their hands, feeling a compulsion to include herself in the news of the day. If she had been an actress, the suspicion would have remained in force.

"What did he look like?"

She closed her eyes. "I can still see him."

"You feeling better?"

"I'm okay."

Richard had Maggie bring in the identikit people. He unobtrusively placed a small tape recorder on the table beside the bed, and said, "I want to hear all about it. Total recall. Everything you remember about it, the circumstances, what you did."

"I'll tell you one thing. My takeoff was a lot better than my landing."

"You walked away from it."

"Well, sort of. Should I begin with the nuns?"

"You can skip that part for now. But I am curious."

"She is your sister? Kimberly? Your sister sister."

"That is my boast."

6

Directors of other library systems envied Joanne her vast and affluent domain in Schaumburg, although she knew how people joked about the suburb because it had grown up pell-mell and every which way, all seemingly overnight. Joanne had come when this process was well under way so she had to take on faith the rural paradise that allegedly had been destroyed by a ruthless progress. One of the effects of this was that, even with low rates and scads of industrial exemptions, the tax base was such that money was lavished on the library. And Joanne—née Heit but Mendoza by marriage—thanks to the mood of the times, was made director her second year in the system when her predecessor, Wurms, ran away to the Yucatan with his secretary.

The speed with which she was promoted plus the unstated assumption that she became director for ethnic reasons, had taken the edge off the joy her ascendancy brought to her, and Jorge and the kids. Jorge was an anesthesiologist and the kids, in a genetic lark, were blonds, Maureen and Stella, and redheads, Maurice and Mark. Already the children were benefitting from quotas in a way unneeded by their talents. Jorge would have liked to denounce such special treatment, but held back because he thought he might harm someone genuinely in need of a break.

There were eighty-seven employees in the main library and another seventeen in the branch. Joanne's budget was something she was never specific about with her opposite numbers in other systems, but she was queen of a domain. However, to say that the crown rested uneasily on her head would be to voice her great secret. In her heart of hearts, she felt she had not deserved to be named director, she knew at least a dozen people who were better qualified. She felt it when she moved through the library, visiting this department and that. She always greeted others cheerfully, always striving to be on the best of terms, feeling nonetheless that in her wake she left deep resentment.

She had never told anyone this. To tell Jorge would have reopened old wounds. They had met when Joanne, a graduate of the College of Martha and Mary, having gone on to Illinois for a library degree, was interning in Chicago while he was interning at Cook County Hospital. She had never had the least notion of what prejudice was like until they began to go out. She was appalled, the more so because Jorge had learned to live with it. He was determined to answer such condescension with performance. Even blacks were prejudiced against Hispanics. Jorge, who came from a cultivated and wealthy Puerto Rican family, was considered little better than an illiterate wetback.

Like their father, the children responded to the admittedly diminished prejudice they encountered with a determination to excel. It was an irony of their situation that Joanne, German and Irish in descent, looked more Latin than her husband and children. She had coal black hair from her Irish mother and an olive complexion from her Alsatian father.

All these things, combined with the fact that she was, after all, the boss, made Joanne's life professionally lonely.

Thus it was a great event when she and Astrid Johansen became friends.

Astrid, looking like a Norse chieftain's wife, had shown up in her office one day and announced, "You have none of my books."

It had been a bad day and Joanne was in no mood to placate someone who probably had published a cookbook with her parish society.

"Why don't you leave the information at acquisitions and we'll see what we can do."

"I thought you might say that." Astrid emptied the contents of a cloth bag onto Joanne's desk. "So I am donating these autographed copies to the library." She smiled and the atmosphere altered as if by magic. "I'm new here."

Joanne asked her to sit, she had coffee brought in, she leafed through the books as they talked. The books were not what she might have feared under the circumstances—privately printed poems, a history of her family, or imitation Dr. Seuss—but genuine books, two brought out by a New York publisher and a third by a reputable specialty publisher in Denver.

"We have none of these?"

"No. But neither does the Chicago library." She displayed again the smile that seemed to suggest the northern lights. "Please don't think I have been going around to other libraries like this. I do live in Schaumburg."

"What are you writing now?"

"It's interesting that you should ask that question." The smile; then she talked a bit about her work, but only a bit. She was a confident and apparently talented woman but she did not assume that the world must therefore be interested in anything she might think or say.

No rings suggested marriage and indeed Astrid was no longer married. She had moved from Wisconsin alone after the breakup of her marriage, and her new life would center around what hitherto had been only an avocation, her writing. Phyllis in acquisitions rolled her eyes when Joanne turned the books over to her but two days later said how much she liked them.

"I'm surprised we didn't have one of them at least. Where did you meet her?" Phyllis asked.

"It was completely by accident," Joanne said vaguely.

She was like a high school girl who feared that others might win away her new friend. She wanted to keep Astrid to herself. That is why she did not do the obvious thing, which was ask Astrid to make a presentation in the auditorium. There was a meet-the-author program into which she would have fit, but Joanne didn't mention it and neither did Astrid.

With her honey blond braided hair, her great blue eyes, and large-boned body, Astrid was not someone easily overlooked. If she had come regularly to the library, it would have been only a matter of time before it became known who she was and others would usurp the place Joanne claimed for her own. She had not had a close friend since college and given the complexities of her career she felt a profound need of a confidante. Astrid was not only willing but eager to play that role.

"If you ever imagine that being single is a state of liberation, forget it," Astrid said.

"I'm perfectly happy as I am. Married, I mean."

"You're fortunate. I wonder if my ex-husband finds it as difficult as I do. Everyone my age is married. Of course it's different with men."

"Are you still in touch?"

"No."

Just no. In much the same way, Joanne screened off her professional life from their friendship. It was as if they had met in a strange place and constructed a friendship without the usual antecedents. They met Wednesdays for lunch, they usually hit the malls together on Saturday afternoons;

Astrid was an enthusiastic supporter of the kids' soccer teams and Stella's ballet. Joanne had expected Astrid to be forthcoming about her writing, but the project she was working on was giving her trouble.

"I have parts but no whole. There is the satisfaction of writing and finishing elements but how it will fit together is still unclear. I should add that this kind of procedure is a recipe for disaster. If I could proceed any other way I would."

"I've never written."

"Have you wanted to?"

Joanne thought about it. "Not really. I love books, of course; I read indiscriminately, but, no, I guess I never did feel the urge to write."

Astrid showed little interest in other writers. If she had noticed the publicity put out for visiting authors and shown up for their talks, that would have been understandable. It was one of the possibilities Joanne half feared at first. But Astrid saw writing as a lonely individual effort that gained little from solidarity with others who were doing the same. Nor was she much interested in the other events sponsored by the library. That is why Joanne was surprised when Astrid showed such interest in the lecture by Richard Moriarity.

This had been one of Joanne's inspirations, fueled by the realization that the Richard Moriarity who had been named as chief investigator into the savage slayings of three young women was indeed the brother of the Kimberly Moriarity she knew through her continued friendship with Sister Mary Teresa Dempsey.

Joanne had visited the house on Walton Street only twice, but she and her old history professor exchanged cards and notes and occasional telephone calls. In this Joanne knew she was like hundreds of other alumnae of the college. With the institution itself no more, the fact that there was a living link with it on Walton Street in Chicago assumed even greater importance. It was at Walton Street that she had met Kim.

She did not of course exploit this connection when she had approached Lieutenant Moriarity, but the first time they met, she asked if he and Kimberly were twins.

"She's my little sister," he had said, with obvious affection.

His first reaction to the suggestion that he come out to Schaumburg and talk about the investigation he headed was negative.

"I'm no speaker. And anyway I'd rather wait until I can announce that we've done what we've been asked to do."

"People out our way are terribly concerned, you know."

While none of the murders had been in Schaumburg, they were close. Besides, the suburb had known other unsettling horrors of late. So Joanne pursued the subject—he hadn't said flatly no—and after a while, she found his attitude completely altered.

"I think I will. I've talked about it with members of the team from out there—I have to tell you, I brought it up as a kind of joke—and they think good can come of it. So tell me what you have in mind."

From that point on it had been simply a matter of arrangements, and Joanne kept everything in her own hands. This was her inspiration and she meant to carry it out herself, for good or ill.

"I'll want to hear him," Astrid said at a Wednesday lunch.

"I hope there'll be a good audience." Appearances and talks were chancy things. Joanne could have told Astrid tales. Famous writers came and talked to a handful while flashes in the pan drew full houses. There seemed no way to predict or control such things. Nonetheless, Joanne resolved to bear it all on her own shoulders.

"Is he coming just for the talk?" Astrid asked.

"What do you mean?"

"Will you give him dinner first, or have a reception?"

"If I suggested that I'm afraid he'd back out even now. He seems very shy. Well, sort of shy."

"I'd hoped to get a chance to speak to him."

Astrid had never struck Joanne as the kind of person to surround a speaker and gush and say how marvelous it was, even when one didn't understand a thing and probably had no intention of reading the speaker's books. Even minor celebrity exercises a powerful attraction and there are some who find it irresistible. Surely Astrid wasn't at all like that.

But on the night of the talk—and it was a triumph, Joanne could not have been more pleased, this single event seemed to vindicate her appointment as director, she had put on the event of the year—on the night of the talk, there was Astrid, unmistakable as a Viking princess, chatting amiably with Richard Moriarity. Joanne's first impression was that they already knew one another. Availing herself of the privileges of the organizer, she joined the two of them. She was startled to hear them making arrangements to meet. Joanne was embarrassed, fearful she had discovered an unsuspected side of her friend.

"We're going to write a book together," Astrid said over coffee the next day when they met to review the triumph of the night before. Joanne had been unable not to tease Astrid about how well she had gotten on with the speaker.

"A book. About what?"

"About the case he's working on. I've just planted the seed, but I am sure he will want me to do it."

When she got used to it, Joanne thought it was a wonderful idea, and it did not lose any of its allure from the thought that her arranging Richard Moriarity's talk had made the project possible.

"I would like to be involved in the investigation, to work at his side and see it all. I could write it so much more vividly if that can be arranged."

It sounded unlikely to Joanne but she said nothing to diminish Astrid's enthusiasm.

"His sister is a nun, you know."

"How would I know that?"

"Because I'm telling you. She belongs to the order that ran the college I attended. There is just a remnant left, living in a house in Chicago. I must take you there sometime."

"To a convent!"

"Astrid, it's unlike any convent you have ever seen."

"No, it isn't. I've never seen any convent ever."

"Then you have a treat in store for you."

"Lucky me," Astrid murmured ironically.

7

Katherine Senski was not the kind of woman who sought to diminish the effect of her height by favoring low heels or a stopped posture. She gloried in her size, magnifying it with a dramatic mode of dress which seemed to recall earlier fashion, although she had been as eccentric in her youth as now in what she preferred to think of as her fully mature years. She wore hats when almost no one did and she went bareheaded when hats were in style. She favored flowing garments, wrappers over long skirts of late, and jewelry, lots of jewelry, for ornamentation, not as a display of wealth. She haunted auctions and out-of-the-way stores for pieces that were unlike anything anyone else was wearing. She was a determined individualist.

It was this that had drawn her all those years ago to her friend and (a term she relished in this connection) co-eval, Sister Mary Teresa Dempsey. As the premiere newswoman of her time, and still active in the capacity of special reporter for the *Tribune,* Katherine had been a good role model for the students at the College of Martha and Mary. Asked to give the commencement address one year, she performed in a way that became legendary. She was soon on the board of trustees. It was in that capacity, along with Benjamin Rush, a lawyer and fellow member of the board, that she had fought at Emtee Dempsey's side during the long twilight struggle the order went through as the result of the recent and, to Katherine, lamentable ecumenical council. The end result was something less than total defeat—the order remained, even if it was now reduced to three members and one postulant, and some of the property donated by generous friends and alumnae had been preserved from the whims of what seemed determined to be the last generation of the order. Sweetest of all was the retention of the house on Walton Street, her affection for which Katherine had difficulty concealing.

"You should live here, Katherine. It is ridiculous for an old lady like you to be living alone, taking up a vast apartment all by yourself."

"It would be more ridiculous for an inveterate laywoman like myself to take up residence in a convent."

"Inveterate," Emptee Dempsey repeated, with emphasis.

Joyce suggested that Katherine might consider becoming a postulant. "Then we would have a class of two."

"I pray every day that the order may flourish and attract many bright and dedicated women. If I became a postulant I would be preventing my own prayer from being answered."

The conversation went on, Katherine protesting and expostulating but loving it all the same. The prospect of being unable to live alone, unable to care for herself, dwelt on the edge of her mind, a thought she never quite admitted. But when it did get its nose into the tent of her consciousness, she expelled the attendant fear by telling herself she would just move in with her friends on Walton Street.

"I will be drooling out of both sides of my mouth before that happens of course."

"So you are halfway there," Emtee Dempsey said wickedly.

Katherine was a worldly woman and her profession had taken her into the seediest as well as the most sybaritic of environments. She had sat at the bar with her male colleagues and exchanged the rough gossip of the day and had inured herself to the language that often characterized such get-togethers as the night wore on. Nor had she escaped the dart of Eros, a phrase she might have dared use in the early days of her journalistic career. She had fallen in love with a man who loved her too, but they faced the great impediment that he was already married. That was an insuperable obstacle for both of them; they had parted in great sorrow but with equally great resolve. Katherine had been a girl of twenty-nine. It had troubled her conscience that she went on loving a married man, even though they no longer met and had no intention of doing so again.

"Yours is a selfless love, Katherine. What Aquinas calls *amor amicitiae*. It's all in Aristotle, of course. It is because you wish his good and he wishes yours that you have resolved to stop things where you did."

Katherine permitted herself to think that of course the old nun couldn't really understand what it was like. Nonetheless, she had spoken the kind of truth Katherine needed to hear. It would have been false to tell herself she no longer loved the one she loved. That she might love him without wanting him for herself alone was a great relief. It had made life possible for her, however lonely the prospect had seemed.

On this Tuesday morning, still breakfasting, Katherine called Ginger Federstein at the *Tribune*, a girl who had been her protégée and was now one of the most popular columnists on the paper.

"Are you covering the visit of Cecilia Vespertina, Ginger?"

"Oh, am I glad you called. The strangest thing. Her advance person, a girl named Mitzi Earl, was the object of an attempted abduction yesterday. Have you heard?"

"No!"

"We had all agreed to sit on it, but one of the talk shows got going on Oscar and the host just blurted it out," Ginger explained.

"Oscar?"

"It's what we're calling the serial killer. We're playing the story for all it's worth now. Richard Moriarity is beside himself, but what can we do?"

"Where did this attack take place?"

"Over on Walton Street. She had been—"

"Walton Street! Where on Walton Street?"

"She had just come from a visit to those nun friends of yours."

"My God in heaven. I'm coming down."

"I hoped you'd say that."

The *Tribune* building was the same. So much about the paper was just as it always had been, but Katherine, despite all the years she had pushed through the revolving doors, often felt now that she was a stranger, almost an intruder. The redoubtable Colonel McCormick had owned the paper when she began, and he'd ruled it with an iron if whimsical hand. When at last he was gone, may he rest in peace, they could write English correctly again. The colonel, like George Bernard Shaw, had come into the grips of the idea that English spelling should be made more congruous with its pronunciation. An approved list of neologisms guided the writing of everyone on the paper. When Katherine heard complaints about the present owner, she held her tongue. The past unknown or forgotten can easily be made to seem better than it was; Katherine knew that, on the whole, things had improved at the paper.

It was the absence of any familiar faces from when she

was young that struck her now. It is a strange feeling to out-live one's contemporaries, or at least outwork them. Retir-ing, she maintained, was something for the wheels of au-tomobiles, not for human beings, or if for human beings, not for journalists. Such thoughts were not for dwelling on, needless to say, and were swept away by the smell and bus-tle of the building.

Ginger, when Katherine looked in on her, was on the phone and at the same time pecking at the keyboard of her computer with the fingers of her free hand. She indicated she would like Katherine to wait. Humming encourage-ment into the phone, she swiveled her monitor so Kather-ine could read what she was writing.

It was headed ADVANCE WOMAN GETS UNWANTED ADVANCE and was Ginger's column for the day. Katherine doubted that the title would survive, then doubted her doubt. Columnists were given greater latitude now and were all but free from editorial excisions and corrections.

Into the phone, Ginger said, "I understand all that and I sympathize, but you're the news now, sweetie, not her. I'll do all I can for her tomorrow, but today you're it."

The conversation soon ended. "That was Mitzi Earl, the woman Oscar tried to grab."

Katherine had considered calling Walton Street before coming to the office, but there was a chance they hadn't even heard of this yet and Katherine wanted to know a good deal more than she did before talking to Emtee Dempsey.

"You're making that assumption about Oscar, or do we know?"

"It's a darned good guess."

"And I know you'll characterize it that way. Tell me, be-fore I burst, what happened to the girl?"

Ginger, as was her way, was colorful and dramatic in her account. Imagining this happening just outside the door of the house on Walton Street filled Katherine with anger. Up to now she had thought of this madman as a scourge of the suburbs and it was a welcome thought that some forms of violence have yet to be urbanized.

"Why was she there, Katherine?" Ginger asked when she was done.

"Running interference for Cecilia Vespertina, who has got it into her head that she wants to talk with some real live nuns. 'How have nuns survived after the consciousness of women has been raised?' That is an exact quote, whether from her or her advance girl I don't know."

"But she's just here on a visit."

"She's always somewhere on a visit. The woman lives the life of a nomad. Chicago seemed as good a place as any and when Mitzi Earl heard about Sister Mary Teresa that decided it. They assumed that any nun would be flattered to have her life inquired into by such a popular author."

"It isn't going to happen?"

"I advised against it. I shall be even more emphatic today. The less attention drawn to the house on Walton Street the better. What an animal this Oscar must be."

"Be careful. Animal righters might object."

"And with reason. A man whose reason is the slave of his passions is worse than an animal."

"Say that again," Ginger said, fingers poised over the keyboard. "I'll give you credit."

"Credit Socrates. I think I stole it from him."

"Who's Socrates?"

For a moment the world reeled, planets threatened to escape their orbits, meteors were poised to rain destruction on the earth.

"Just kidding," Ginger cried when she saw the look on Katherine's face.

"Don't do that to an old lady."

"He runs that Greek restaurant over on State, doesn't he?"

Katherine flounced off to her own office. She knew she

was regarded as the local representative of the bureau of standards, but so be it. Emtee Dempsey often spoke of the way in which monasteries in the Dark Ages became the repositories of such learning as had survived from antiquity.

"For centuries they didn't do much with it. Oh, they made copies of the manuscripts and traded them for things they didn't have. But a long time passed before they did the sort of thinking recorded in the manuscripts. Not that we dare condescend to them," the old nun added sharply. "Just staying alive was more of a job for them than it is for us. Anyway, our time bears striking similarities to theirs. Our records of the past are magnificent, but who now knows of them, or understands them?"

Katherine picked up the phone with the sense that she would be continuing a lifelong conversation.

8

When Lois asked if Kim had heard that Richard was writing a book and Kim cried, "A book! Richard?" Kim feared she had offended her sister-in-law, the last thing in the world she wanted to do. Kim regarded Lois as the best assurance of salvation Richard had. The men in the Moriarity family had been what her mother had somewhat sardonically called cut-ups, exempting Kim's father, but making it clear enough what had made the difference in his case. Having taken on with her mother's milk the conviction that male Moriaritys require a strong uplifting female presence, Kim had always thanked God Richard had found Lois. Among Lois's strongest traits was an unwillingness to suffer any criticism of Richard, apart from her own.

"And why shouldn't he write a book? He seems to have spent half his life writing reports."

"Lois, I think it's wonderful. It's just that I had no idea."

"Neither did he until someone suggested it," Lois admitted, placated. "Have you ever heard of Astrid Johansen?"

"The woman who wrote a book on the Kensington Rune stone?"

"You've heard of her?"

"What about her?" Kim was bewildered by the conversation as it jumped all over the place.

"She's the one who came up with the idea of Richard writing a book about this terrible case he's working on. She heard him speak the other night in Schaumburg and came up afterward and, well, it looks like they're going to collaborate on a book."

"Why doesn't he write it himself?" Kim said, in an apparent reversal of field.

"That's what I said! But he's probably right that he can't do it while he is directing this task force, and after that's done with he will be doing something else. So your brother is going to be an author."

When Kim gave the news to Emtee Dempsey, she warned the old nun not to express surprise when Richard told them.

"I will be happy not to express surprise as soon as he tells me. When can we expect to see him?" Emtee Dempsey asked.

"I'm sure he's busy finding out as much as he can from Mitzi Earl."

Emtee Dempsey's brow darkened at this reminder of the awful deed that almost had been committed outside their doorway. The fact that it was Katherine Senski who had made them aware of the event had not made it easier for the old nun to hear of it. Mitzi's near miss was sufficient to make her feel that her own hospitality had been called into question and the old nun seemed about to begin a personal crusade in pursuit of the man she refused to call Oscar.

"I have known two splendid gentlemen named Oscar in my life," she humphed. "One of them was my father. I refuse to disgrace the name by applying it to this monster. Call him John Doe if you must; that at least has legal precedent."

"Your father's name was Oscar?"

"Is that a smile on your face, Sister Kimberly?"

"I hope not."

"I realize that some names, for no semantic or syntactic or etymological reason, take on comic overtones. This follows on the accident of usage. The man who was my father might easily have been called Austin or Maurice, recurring names in our family, but he was given the name Oscar at his baptism because of an admired friend of my grandfather's. It is a name he will wear for all eternity. . . . "

She was in full swing now and there was nothing to do but ride it out. Kim could hardly wait to tell Joyce what Emtee Dempsey's father's name had been, expecting a joyful hoot at the news, even while she nodded through the old nun's homily on the unfairness involved in finding any proper name in itself somehow comic.

"In any case, it is obvious what I shall want you to do, Sister Kimberly," said the old nun. "However, it will have to wait until after the Websters have been here."

"Of course I'll stay for that," Kim said, not out of eagerness but out of a sense of duty. One of the horrors of recent events was the revelation, made in a phone call that morning, that among the dead girls, the victims of Oscar, was Liz Webster, the daughter of an alumna of Martha and Mary. Coming on the heels of the news of what had happened to Mitzi Earl on their very doorstep, this brought Richard's case to the house on Walton Street in an agonizing way. The other night at dinner they had heard of the case from the viewpoint of an investigator; today they would hear of it from the point of view of a victim.

Graduates of the college had married well—ability to define the adverb was one of the attainments of being educated there—and Anne Webster was no exception. Her husband was also materially well off, the owner of a dozen franchise food places as well as a successful insurance agency. Their faith was strong but nothing had prepared them for the horror when their daughter disappeared and they had endured five weeks of agony, not knowing whether she was dead or alive, until her mangled remains were found, tossed disdainfully into a ditch beside a little-traveled tertiary road.

"We're glad that the police are pooling their resources and going at it systematically," Greg Webster said. "It's about time."

"But it makes the pain fresh again. I suppose it will never go away."

"Would you want it to?" Sister Mary Teresa asked.

They were seated in the living room, the Websters on one of the two facing couches in front of the fireplace, Kim across from them. Sister Mary Teresa was in the brocade chair she favored, though her feet didn't quite reach the floor. The visit had called upon Emtee Dempsey's contemplative resources, since there was nothing of a practical kind she could provide for the Websters. But of course they had not come for that.

"When I read of that attack just outside the door here I told Greg that we had to come see you," Anne said. "I should have come before."

"I had no idea you were enduring such a trial at first, Anne. If I were being quizzed on former students' married names I would have come up with yours easily. But seeing Webster in the paper did not, I am ashamed to say, ring a bell. Thank God you've come now."

"The police don't want us to talk about it, but that dreadful man sends us things." Anne Webster could not hold back a sob.

"Things that belonged to Liz," her husband said, putting his arm about her.

"Clothing?"

They both nodded.

"Dear God."

"She was a good girl," Anne Webster said, but there was

something less than confidence in her voice. Kim's mind went in one direction, but the old nun discerned the mother's anguish.

"She was a student at the University of Chicago?"

"Her test scores went through the ceiling," Greg Webster said. "She began the university before her seventeenth birthday."

"We would have preferred a Catholic school," Anne said, her tone the same.

"That is not always a clear advantage nowadays," Emtee Dempsey said. "Parents have to take full responsibility for the religious education of their children."

"We did our best."

"Sister, when this happened she was going through a phase."

The old nun nodded. "It happens at that age, particularly when a young person first becomes aware of the excitement of education. It can seem as if study is meant to remove mystery. If that's so, how does one hang on to a mystery as if it can survive the advance of knowledge?"

"She never rejected the faith outright," Anne said, a tremor in her voice.

"The one thing we can be sure of is the mercy of God, Anne. Don't presume to know the state of your daughter's soul. I don't know the state of mine half the time. Neither did St. Paul. Pray for her in complete confidence in the goodness of God. She is in our prayers, of course."

"Oh how I wish the college had still been operating, Sister. I would have felt so much better if she'd been going to school there."

"Now don't get me started on that," Emtee Dempsey said, getting started on that, and soon she had led the conversation from the agony of personal loss to the idiotic decisions that had led to the closing of the college.

"I don't see how it could have happened with you opposing it, Sister."

"Sometimes I think it might have survived if I hadn't inspired my opponents to ever wilder efforts."

When Anne began to reminisce about her unforgettable days at the college, Emtee Dempsey beamed and Kim excused herself. Mitzi had agreed to talk with her in the coffee shop off the lobby of the Palmer House.

"I'm beginning to understand Cecilia a little better," Mitzi said when they were seated at a table. "It's not just that I've had my five minutes of fame. Now that I have a taste of what notoriety is, I can see it is totally intangible. On the one hand, you're interviewed by everybody, written up, flashed on TV, and on the other I can walk as anonymously through the lobby as anyone else. No wonder Cecilia has a tendency to want to draw attention to herself constantly. Attention is so fitful she always knows what it would be like if it weren't there at all."

"I should have told you that I report everything almost verbatim to Emtee Dempsey when I get back to Walton Street. She'll love that."

"Emtee?"

"Her initials. As Joyce says, she may be Emtee but she was a full professor, and we know what they're full of."

"I never met anyone quite like her. You have to realize that for me it was like meeting a Buddhist nun might be for you, or the Dalai Lama—fill in the blank. When I saw the get-up she wears all I could think was what a massacre Cecilia is going to make of this one. I stopped worrying after ten minutes."

Kim put a hand on Mitzi's arm. "You can imagine how we felt when we heard what had happened to you."

"Hey, it wasn't your fault. It wasn't my fault either. This guy can strike whenever he wants. They've got to catch him."

"You saw him?"

Mitzi nodded. "When I vaulted over the door, I used my left hand as a pivot, turning as I did. By clock time, it might not even registered, but when I rotated I was looking him right in the eye. It's a face I'll never forget. I've seen the face they put together from my descriptions and it is very close."

"You must have been terrified."

"Only later. At the time I was mad as hell. It was like getting fouled in a sport. Your instinct is to reply in kind. Until I looked into his face all I was thinking of was what I was going to do to whoever tried to shove me into that car."

"Was someone behind the wheel?"

"I don't know."

"Was he going to take you somewhere, do you suppose?"

"He couldn't have done much more there. His maneuver depended on speed and execution. Like a burglar who spends only minutes in a house he's broken into before he's out of there? Even if I hadn't gone over the car the way I did, I think putting up a struggle would have been enough. There were other people on the sidewalk."

"You certainly recovered quickly."

"What does Emtee Dempsey want to know?"

"How old was he?"

Mitzi's shoulders lifted. "Thirty. In his thirties. He could have been forty. I don't know."

"Caucasian?"

"You mean non-minority?" Her eyes twinkled. "Okay, he was Caucasian."

Kim told Mitzi what the Websters had said about receiving items of their daughter's clothing at regular intervals since her body was found.

"Oh no!"

"I don't mean to alarm you, Mitzi, but I was surprised you weren't being guarded."

"Oh, they're around somewhere."

"Police?"

"Three in all. They'll provide me with protection for as

54

long as I'm in town. I'm not worried. I almost wish he'd show his face again."

"At least he can't send you anything."

"He can if he took my scarf. I lost that in the struggle and they didn't find it on the scene. It was only when I was in the cab, heading here, that I realized I didn't have it. My nicest scarf, silk, a mile long, electric blue. I'll miss it."

"Emtee Dempsey told me to tell you to bring Cecilia Vespertina to the house."

"She's agreeing to be interviewed?" Mitzi sounded disappointed.

"As a favor to you."

"I almost wish she'd told Cecilia to go fly a kite. Know what one of the bonuses of all this excitement has been? Cecilia is mad because she thinks I am taking the spotlight from her."

"You're kidding."

"She's delayed her arrival for a day and a half, in the hope that I will fade from the news. I am to stay very much in the background when she alights."

"Why do you work for her?"

"Because it's going to feel so good when I stop."

Benjamin Rush, the sidewalk is a public thoroughfare," Emtee Dempsey told the distinguished lawyer. "It belongs to the city. Do you think we are personally responsible for paving it and keeping it in good repair?"

"Sister, we live in litigious times. I share your disbelief that one's fellow citizens are on the alert for opportunities to bring suit against anyone. You and I remember a time when this would have been unheard of. Not because it was legally impossible to do so, but because it was socially, I might even say, morally unacceptable."

"The young woman isn't a fellow citizen. She's just visiting the city."

"I read the papers, Sister. I know what you know."

"If you read the papers you know what they know, but not what I know."

Far from taking umbrage at the pugnacity of the old nun, Benjamin Rush was delighted to find her in such fine form. His concern that she might be sued by Mitzi Earl because of the attempted assault on her on the sidewalk in front of the house on Walton Street was not exaggerated. She and he might lament this, but as her lawyer he could not omit telling her this.

"What exactly would the charge be?"

"You released her without warning into a dubious street in a city notorious for violence and crime."

"Dubious?"

"I speak as her attorney might."

"Then you are not lending your considerable linguistic authority to the notion that dubious could modify street. Dubitable, perhaps, capable of inspiring doubt."

"Why not doubtful street?"

"I am not, as you know, a purist, but such usage has an anthropomorphic tinge to it in my mind."

There was, of course, method in her madness and, much as he enjoyed the pyrotechnics of her conversation, Benjamin Rush could see that she found painful what had happened outside her door to Mitzi Earl, and he said as much.

"Painful, Benjamin Rush. Painful?" She stirred in her chair and her headdress shook in response to the emotion she felt. "That is far too inadequate to express what I feel. What I *think*. Some would call my thought paranoid, but I will risk the displeasure of an old friend and lay it out for you."

For the next few minutes, Benjamin Rush listened with growing dismay to the old nun's brief that recent events would reveal their significance only when they were seen in their relation to the Order of Martha and Mary.

Item. Forget chronology and start with the event that had brought Rush today. Mitzi Earl is attacked outside the house on Walton Street where she had been on a mission on behalf of her employer Cecilia Vespertina.

Item. Cecilia Vespertina, celebrated author of books whose aim is essentially the same as that of the once more than equally popular Couéism ("Every day in every way things are getting better and better," repeated as what would now be called a mantra), decides she must interview Sister Mary Teresa Dempsey, of all the nuns in the world.

Item. Liz Webster, one of the girls killed by John Doe, the so-called serial killer, was the daughter of an alumna of the order's school.

The little nun sat ticking off these items, tapping the pad of the extended thumb of one hand with the index finger of the other, frowning fiercely into the middle distance as she did so. Now the finger was suspended above the thumb as she fell silent, seeking to find a way to add other happenings to these on the thread of her obsession. Benjamin Rush's heart fell and sadness came over him.

He feared it in himself, he looked for it in his contemporaries, he had been certain that Sister Mary Teresa would be the last to succumb, but he worried that he was witnessing the beginning of the decay of a great mind. Charles De Gaulle called old age a shipwreck and Benjamin Rush, who had sailed Lake Michigan since he was a boy, found the metaphor apt. He had known Sister Mary Teresa in her strength when, to take a biblical metaphor, she had been like an army drawn up in battle array, of formidable intellect and a character that combined the virtues acquired by years of diligent effort with those gifts of the spirit that made her far more impressive than the most naturally accomplished woman he had ever known. She was first and foremost a nun, a woman whose life was defined by a resolve to respond to the divine impulse and become saintly. With all her learning and what seemed to him her sanctity, she also possessed remarkable practical acumen. She had perceived the future when it was a cloud no larger than a man's hand and said where the so-called reforms were taking her order.

"It is not new nuns you want to be," she had warned the opposite party, "you don't want to be nuns at all. The new nun is no nun."

Typically she had caught the problem in a phrase. At the time, her adversaries in the order were appalled.

Doubtless many thought they were simply implementing what Vatican II had said about the renewal of religious orders.

"Religious orders should be renewed by recapturing their original charism or inspiration," Sister Mary Teresa reminded the others. "Has a committee been appointed to make a historical study of the wishes and writings of the Blessed Abigail in this regard?"

Rush had been privy to this quarrel to the degree that it had spilled over into meetings of the board of the college. He had been amazed at the proposals that were made for the order. Their lives were being wasted, it was said, educating daughters of the middle class so that they could move up higher on the socioeconomic scale. The poor should be the object of their efforts. From a laudable sense of the undeniable claim of the poor upon them had come a decision to close down the college and sell off the order's property. The counterproposal that more scholarships be added to include the daughters of the poor in the student body were dismissed as tokenism or worse, as recruiting new members for the exploiting class.

The college was closed, the property sold for a risible sum which was then dispersed to small groups of sisters living in apartments. How much of that money ever helped the poor? Once they had begun kicking over the traces of their vocation as they themselves had lived it, most members of the order followed the logic of their position to what Sister Mary Teresa had from the outset claimed it was: They simply ceased to be nuns.

The battle became one of organized retreat and Rush was proud that he had played some role in retaining this house on Walton Street as a fallback position—if it had come to that, he would have bought the property and deeded it back to the remaining nuns—as well as a lakeshore place in Michigan.

Such thoughts paraded through his mind as he listened to what could only be described as a pathetic effort on his old friend's part to understand recent, farflung events in terms of her own sequestered life. He forbore asking her how the other victims of the killer fit into this scheme, instead seeking desperately for a way to turn her from an obsession that would be derided by anyone who heard it.

"The rest will become clear," the old nun finally said, letting her hands fall into her lap. "In the meantime, keep this to yourself, Benjamin. It would be premature to put it forward at this time."

"If you think that is the best course."

"Don't you agree?"

"I think you are right. I myself have difficulty seeing just where your hypothesis leads."

"Well then, we shall for the nonce keep it to ourselves. I have however made a similar suggestion to Katherine Senski. You might make it clear to her that she should not publicize it yet."

Benjamin Rush nodded. In response to the old nun's question as to what he expected her to do about his fear that suit might be brought against her for what had happened to Mitzi Earl on the walk outside, he suggested that he prepare a suit against the city for failing to provide proper safeguards and security, etc., etc. He saw that his proposal received from her a reaction not unlike his own to her great conspiracy theory. But he could cite cases of the kind he feared. In the new world of the law there are no accidents, there are only victims and villains. In that world it was all one could do to shift villain status from oneself to the public at large.

Before he left, Margaret Mary brought in tea, and Sister Mary Teresa, suddenly back in form, asked the postulant to join them. Her family was well known to Benjamin

Rush and he asked about her siblings. He nodded with the pleasure of the aged to her report on her brothers, whom he had known as children.

"And Bridget? What is Bridget doing?"

Margaret Mary's bright expression faded. "She was the first of us to die, Mr. Rush."

"I'm so sorry. I hadn't heard."

"She had moved to Minnesota."

"Ah." It might have been Ultima Thule, only a few hundred miles to the northwest of where they sat.

When she had taken away the things and Rush was preparing to go, Sister Mary Teresa whispered that it was the death of her sister and husband that had turned Margaret Mary's thoughts to religion.

"A spur, perhaps, but not a motivation. She is a tad too lugubrious still."

"Ah well, she's Irish."

"Oh, I'm making allowances. We will see, we will see."

In his car he talked to Katherine Senski, having his driver make the call. He found it difficult to carry on a conversation in a moving car, observed by other motorists. It seemed affected. The suggestion that he have tinted glass installed did not appeal. He would feel he was riding in a hearse.

Katherine asked him to stop by.

"You've been given tea, I'll wager," she said, standing in the open door of her apartment, watch in hand, when he emerged from the elevator.

"I have."

"Then I shall offer you more substantial refreshment."

"Have any Irish whisky, perhaps?"

"Jameson."

"Wonderful."

In the background Katherine's radio was tuned to a station that broadcast only classical music and they sat high above the frantic and sometimes violent activity of the city listening to Bach fugues. It was a good atmosphere in which to discuss their mutual friend.

"She specifically asked that we keep her theory quiet."

"Theory," Katherine said sadly. "It was all I could do not to weep when she started on it."

"Her mind seemed clear when I left."

"It is just a lapse, I'm sure. Perhaps I should speak with Sisters Kimberly and Joyce to see if they have noticed anything?"

Rush was reminded of the constitutional provision that a president who becomes mentally ill is to be replaced by the vice president, a seemingly straightforward line of action. The great difficulty lay in determining the president's condition. Were he himself to be the judge, he would have to be sane enough to see that he was mad. For the vice president to do it threatened a usurpation of powers. To leave it in the hands of doctors was already to transfer authority before the fact.

"But I am boring you."

"I see the analogy, Benjamin."

"If it is indeed one, the problem is insoluble."

On that note they fell silent, Bach become more audible, the smoothness of the whisky a delight. The ringing of the phone made them both jump. To the jangling of the excessive jewelry she wore on her arms as well as around her throat, Katherine picked up the phone. The message lifted her to her feet.

"No! When? Oh my Lord."

Benjamin Rush was in a quandary. He could not pretend not to hear her end of this obviously upsetting call. He rose and looked around as a man in search of the plumbing looks around. To his surprise Katherine signaled for him to stay. She covered the phone.

"Mitzi Earl is dead. Strangled."

She lifted her hand and demanded more information. Benjamin Rush fought the relief he had felt to learn that the news was not about the dear old friend they had just been discussing.

10

The trio that had been on guard at the Palmer House seemed to be in a state of shock when Richard asked them how anyone could have gotten to that girl while they were on duty.

"We don't know how she got downstairs," Zeke Bowler said.

"She had to be trying to give us the slip," Kitty Carr said. "You're bound to look away every once in a while."

Dave Dillon wisely kept his mouth shut. Obviously none of them knew how Mitzi Earl got strangled on the basement level of the hotel. They all had been upstairs watching an empty room.

"When did you last see her?" Richard asked, trying to be patient.

If they had it right, Carr had seen her last, at eight-fifteen when she had come back from breakfast. Carr had her under surveillance on the elevator down, and in the restaurant she'd had a clear view of Mitzi Earl at all times.

"She had French toast," she added, as if in proof. Well, he'd rather hear it from her than from the pathologist.

The main lobby of the hotel was on the first floor European style, the second floor American. The entrance on street level gave onto a concourse that ran from State to

Randolph streets. An escalator went up to the lobby. From the concourse an escalator also descended to the basement where there were shops and the restaurant in which Mitzi Earl had French toast for her last breakfast on earth.

While Kitty Carr had the subject under surveillance, Bowler and Dillon were on the alert for suspicious-looking characters trying to get to the floor she was on. Her room had been changed since the assault on Walton Street and no one at the desk would have given out its number, though Richard wanted to talk to everyone on the desk this morning. And the bellboys.

The manager in charge was named Feely and he looked steadily at Richard as if waiting for him to comment. Imagine going through life with a name like that. Think of all the bad jokes he had had to bear. At thirty or so, Feely had a haughty bearing, spoke with great formality, and might just as well have had an electric fence around him.

"No, sir," he said, when Richard asked him if it were possible that anyone at the desk could have told anyone where Miss Earl was staying.

"You've talked with them all?"

"I know what their instructions were."

"And they would never ignore instructions?"

"Not and remain employees at this hotel, sir."

"I wish I had your kind of confidence in those working for me."

"I understand there was a breakdown in security."

"Yeah."

Windtheiser, the bell captain, was five and a half feet tall and stood on his left leg with his right hand inserted into the double-breasted jacket of his uniform. His smile was the smile of a man who has seen it all. His black hair was slicked down on his head. He looked as if he was the dreaming conqueror in the years ere he saw Elba.

"Anything is possible, Captain."

"Lieutenant." Richard was glad he was in civvies. Windtheiser might have saluted a fellow officer—or been waiting to receive a salute. After all, he was a captain. His troops lounged around a pulpitlike stand that nestled against a pillar just behind the check-in counter. Mercenaries, what would they not do for money? Richard went over to them with Windtheiser at his side, as if they were about to inspect the troops.

"Which of you did the reporter talk to?"

They looked at one another. It was like fishing in a chlorinated pool, a cast made without hope but knowing, like Windtheiser, that anything is possible.

A blond with Adams on his nameplate, tall enough to be a basketball player, cleared his throat. "I told her we couldn't answer questions like that."

Bingo. "So she just went away?"

"Oh, she kept after me." He reached into his pocket and brought out a twenty-dollar bill. He grinned. "She gave me this."

"For not telling her anything?"

"I didn't tell her."

"So what did you do for the twenty dollars?"

Snickering started among his fellows. Windtheiser snapped his fingers and they stopped. Adams said, "I said I'd bring a note to Miss Earl."

"And you did?"

Adams said he had gone up on the elevator, got off on the fourth floor, waited a while, and then came down.

"Was the reporter still here when you came down?"

"Why would she be?"

Richard looked up at the balcony that ran around the lobby area. Here and there, people stood regarding the activity below. From several points on that balcony, Adams could have been seen entering an elevator.

"Where can Adams and I have a talk?" he asked Windtheiser.

"Our life is lived in the public eye," Windtheiser said theatrically.

Richard asked Adams to show him exactly how he had taken the note to Mitzi Earl's room. Adams looked sheepish.

"I didn't."

"You said the reporter wasn't here when you came down."

"I just went up a couple of floors and after a couple of minutes came down."

"You didn't go to Mitzi Earl's room?"

"No."

"Good boy."

Adams was relieved when he saw Richard wasn't being sarcastic.

"Okay. Was she short or tall, old or young?"

"Tall. She came up to here on me. She wasn't young."

"Are you any good at descriptions?"

"Oh, it's her hair you notice. Kind of yellow and braided, like a little girl's, only it looked right on her, you know?"

A few more questions made it clear that Adams was talking about Richard's literary collaborator. He didn't like it, but he should have expected it. She would probably tell him he should have called her before going over to the Palmer House when he had received the news about Mitzi Earl. He would have arranged an interview with the girl if she had asked him and he sure as hell didn't like the idea that she was creeping around the Palmer House bribing bellboys.

"What did you do with the note?" he asked Adams, and the boy blushed like the adolescent he had only recently been.

"I tossed it."

"Where?"

"I tore it up and flushed it down the john."

"You may have a future in the post office."

When he got down to the basement level, an area maybe twenty-five yards long had been cordoned off and the traffic in and out of the restaurant was slowed by gawkers. With the spots on for the photographers and the body outlined under a blanket, Trunket, the medical examiner, might have been shooting a scene for a movie. He directed his staff with aplomb, greeting Richard with a toothy smile.

"Death by strangulation," he said cheerfully.

"With what?"

"A scarf. Striking thing, long as Paul Bunyan's axe handle, bright, silk." Trunket stepped closer and said in a whisper, "No sense of color, Richard. The scarf clashes with that outfit she has on."

Richard knelt as if to check Trunket's sartorial comment. He lifted the blanket and looked at the surprisingly peaceful final expression of Mitzi Earl. Her throat was bruised and he could still make out the bruises from the assault of the other day. This postman obviously had rung twice.

"Was she carrying a bag?"

"No sign of one."

"How'd you identify her?"

"I didn't. One of those who was supposed to be guarding her made the identification."

Richard got out of the lighted area and noticed the elevators to the left and the stairway to the right. She might have just gotten off the elevator when it happened, or just been getting on. Richard turned and went into the restaurant where he showed Florence the manager his badge.

"That body out there isn't helping business, is it?"

"It is a body then?"

Florence wore a suit and had her hair messed up in the current fashion, but Richard liked her reaction.

"A girl. She had breakfast in here. She was wearing a kind of maroon suede suit."

"With green lapels."

"So you remember her."

"Both times. She had breakfast and then left but came back because she had forgotten her purse. Can you imagine a woman forgetting her purse? It had been turned in to me so I gave it to her."

He thanked Florence and went back to Trunket. "Anything I ought to know unofficially right now?"

"You in charge of this?"

"It's connected with Oscar."

Trunket formed an O with his mouth as if he were about to give an elocution lesson or was imitating a fish out of water.

Going up on the elevator to the room Richard entertained philosophical thoughts. Florence was of course right. Few women go anywhere without their purse. If Mitzi had remembered to take hers when she left the restaurant, she would probably be alive. If she had had the sense to ask Kitty Carr to go back and get it for her, she would be alive. There were so many ways in which she could still be alive, and yet she was lying on the floor of the basement level of the Palmer House dead, no doubt strangled by the same man who had tried to push her into a car on Walton Street.

Inside the room he went immediately to the phone and called Florence in the restaurant.

"How did she pay her bill if she didn't have her purse with her when she left the restaurant?"

"Oh, she signed her room number while still at her table. She paid all right."

Yeah. Richard hung up but kept his hand on the phone, undecided whether to call Astrid or Kim. As if to show his annoyance with Astrid's visit to the Palmer House, he called Walton Street.

Richard, what dreadful news," Kim said. "Sister Mary Teresa has been on her knees in the chapel ever since we heard."

"At least she gave us a good description of him after the first attempt. We're hoping that someone spotted him around the hotel before or after this happened."

"We should have taken Mitzi in here after she was attacked. No one would have expected to find her here."

Richard said nothing and Kim was not really surprised. In the past, when he had followed such a suggestion, he had almost lost control of an investigation because of Sister Mary Teresa's interest. "When will you come tell her all this, Richard?"

"I thought you were her eyes and ears."

"There's no substitute for hearing it from you."

Kim closed her eyes and breathed a little prayer of expiation. Flattering him was something Emtee Dempsey did shamelessly and, as witness, Kim had always resented how malleable her brother was. He said he would call again later in the day and try to drop by before going home.

"Tell her I can't stay for dinner."

It would have been more appropriate to tell Joyce. Kim went into the kitchen and looked a question at Joyce.

"Still in chapel."

Kim went down the hall to the chapel and knelt at her prie-dieu. Earlier Monsignor McCarthy had said Mass for them here, and it was here that they said morning and evening prayers together every day. Margaret Mary was arranging flowers on the altar. There had been a definite aesthetic lift since their new postulant arrived. Oblivious to everything around her, Sister Mary Teresa was sunk in prayer.

When Kim was a novice, Emtee Dempsey had described her mode of mental prayer. "I am being let down gradually deeper and deeper into myself, leaving behind everything that distracts and gets between me and God. I listen. The deeper I descend the more I am freed from myself. Augustine said he wanted to know only two things, God and the soul. He found God within himself, but it was the opposite of self-absorption."

She had other suggestions too, the one Joyce liked was called "not talking to yourself." "Thinking is by and large talking to oneself. When you do this aloud people are apt to be alarmed. Prayer is talking to Jesus, or to Mary, who are closer to us than we are to ourselves. Talk to them."

Joyce often found it difficult not to be audible when she talked to herself but with the presence of Margaret Mary in the house she was less apt to be heard mumbling in the kitchen. She didn't want to frighten their postulant away.

Kim said a prayer for Mitzi Earl, for the repose of her soul, that she might know eternal rest. Mitzi had claimed to have no particular religious beliefs. Maybe talking with Emtee Dempsey had turned her mind to the point of life. It was impossible to think that so vital a person simply had ceased to exist, period, all that curiosity and talent gone now, in retrospect pointless. Not that a person had to be special in order to be destined for eternity.

When Kim left the chapel, Emtee Dempsey was still deep in prayer. Margaret Mary had left earlier and was now in what they were calling the computer room. She had brought with her a powerful desktop computer with a huge hard disk as well as a CD-ROM drive. Emtee Dempsey had okayed the project Margaret Mary proposed with some skepticism that it was possible: the creation of a database that would include all the records of the college now stored in file cabinets in the basement of the house.

"Typing it in would make it formidably difficult, but scanning it is easy," Margaret Mary explained. "Boring but easy."

"I think Sister imagines this will be a life's work. Is it?"

"It'll take months."

"Is that all?"

"Do you think that's overly optimistic?"

"Mimi, I have no idea. I can drive a car and use a computer but I haven't any real understanding of what makes them work."

"It's quite simple."

Margaret Mary had the look of someone about to give a seminar on computer hardware. Kim got her back onto the college database.

"Sister Mary Teresa," she began, then stopped, then whispered, "When do I get to call her Emtee Dempsey?"

"To her face? Never."

"Oh, I wouldn't."

"What were you going to say?"

"She asked me to begin at the end, with the latest years, and work backward. It doesn't matter. I could just choose files at random and enter them. The access program will determine what is brought up."

Kim knew that it was the old nun's ambition, if she ever finished her history of the twelfth century, to write a history of the college, up to but not including the quarrels that brought about its demise.

"Someone should write that story too," she had once suggested.

"Someone who was not a protagonist, Sister Kimberly," Emtee Dempsey added. "I will leave that to you."

Despite the tragic news about Mitzi, the old nun had done her allotted number of pages that day. Her scholarly work was part of her vocation and she approached it with a sense of duty as well as joy. Then she had gone to chapel.

When Kim came out of the computer room, the old nun was emerging from chapel, blessing herself with great precision.

"Richard called, Sister."

"Come tell me about it."

Sister Mary Teresa moved slowly down the hallway, seeming to use her cane more than usual. She said over her shoulder, "Why does an old wreck like me live on when the young are cut down before they've had a chance to live?"

A rhetorical question, but one indicative of the grief the old nun felt. She would not normally speak as if one death could be exchanged for another.

She listened to Kim's account of what Richard had said. "Because she went back for her purse!"

"It's perfectly understandable."

"Of course it is. An ordinary action that a person should be able to perform without risk of harm. But she was being stalked by this dreadful man, there is no doubt of that. If he had not caught her there he would have persisted until he caught her somewhere else."

"But she was under guard. She was supposed to have protection as long as she was in town, and then she would leave."

"And what does her dreadful employer have to say to all this?"

"She arrives today."

"I thought she was due before then."

"She was. She postponed it because she thought what had happened to Mitzi would dull the impact she hopes to make. Maybe she'll postpone her visit entirely now."

The phone rang and when Kim picked it up it was Joyce. "Turn on Channel Nine. Cecilia Vespertina is on."

Emtee Dempsey nodded when Kim told her what it was and Kim went into the sun porch and turned on the set, with the old nun following.

Cecilia had just deplaned and was being interviewed in the VIP lounge at O'Hare, the first event in the itinerary Mitzi had planned for her. Attention had been paid to lighting, the news services had sent their top crews, and Cecilia in person must have removed all doubts that her arrival was indeed news.

The photographs on the jacket of her book did not do justice to the striking woman. She had a knack for speaking directly into the lens and thus addressing the viewer with an intimacy not often felt in the "on the spot" reports that make up so much of the news. The reporters themselves usually occupied center stage, addressing the audience eye to eye, but the subjects of the news were usually just seen. Not so Cecilia Vespertina. She wore what Katherine would have called a cloche hat that emphasized the size and shape of her head, her generous profile with its great dramatic nose seemed to call for new standards of feminine beauty, and her face was the most expressive Kim had ever seen. The slightest alteration of the line of her mouth as she listened to a question affected the viewer like a primal shout. Her mouth made her basic expression that of a tragic mask. She had come to Chicago not in triumph, but in mourning, as her assistant had been murdered that very morning by a wild beast who went about seeking whom he might devour.

"I do not blame your city for this outrage. It is the sort of thing women have come to expect anywhere, and everywhere. What are women supposed to think of themselves when there are beasts who see them only as prey, to be possessed, ravished, and then discarded?"

Emtee Dempsey was as spellbound as Kim. There was no running commentary as was usually the case when the old nun watched television. She still stood, leaning on her cane, hanging on every word that Cecilia spoke.

"I have come here to speak, to guide, to counsel, yes. But I have another purpose as well, a purpose from which I shall not be deflected by the tragic loss of my devoted assistant. In these days when women at long last are rising to the expectations planted in their nature, when they are freeing themselves from the male standards that have been imposed upon them for centuries, there are women among us who represent one of the great historical achievements of our gender. From time immemorial, such women have formed communities of their own, self-governed, autonomous. Men entered there to the degree that they did on the terms of the community. This tradition continues among us and is ignored by what is pleased to call itself the Women's Movement. While I am in Chicago I shall have the enormous privilege of visiting with Sister Mary Teresa Dempsey, a world-renowned scholar, in order that she might instruct me on the lives she and her sisters live."

With that she dismissed the press, wading through them with an indifference verging on contempt. The station returned to one of the daily soap operas and Kim turned it off.

"She managed that whole performance without once mentioning Mitzi Earl by name."

"Well, she mentioned your name."

"Did she not? And I will see her too, I will definitely see her. This woman is difficult to understand but I know she has her part in the scheme."

Kim's heart sank. Katherine had passed on to her the concern she and Mr Rush shared about Emtee Dempsey. On no basis that anyone could see, the old nun was convinced that the dreadful events unrolling around them did not simply impinge upon the order and the house on

75

Walton Street, but that their true meaning and import could only be found in their relation to the Order of Martha and Mary. It was very difficult for Kim to reassure Katherine.

"You know how she is."

"But I also knew how she was. This is decline, Sister Kimberly, this is decline."

"I have thought so before and been wrong," Kim said.

"And you have whistled past many graveyards too, I am sure."

The itinerary for Cecilia Vespertina's visit, which Mitzi had given Kim the last time they talked, had the author coming to Walton Street at ten o'clock the following morning. Kim went into the kitchen to tell Joyce.

"At that hour, what's the worry?"

"She may not have had breakfast. It's unclear. We are the first item on the agenda for tomorrow. Did Mitzi say she slept late?"

"Poor Mitzi," Joyce said. "Did you know she played volleyball for Pepperdine?"

There were remarks of Joyce's that Kim did not pretend to understand, and this was one of them. Her rule was to ignore them.

"Have rolls in case, but coffee for sure."

"Does she look like a coffee drinker to you?"

"Have juice as well."

"Laced with cyanide?"

"Joyce."

"She didn't even mention Mitzi's name."

"Emtee Dempsey noticed that as well."

I must have been in the hotel when he was there," Astrid said, sipping her espresso.

"Were you asked to be there by Richard Moriarity?" Joanne asked.

Astrid shook her head and her hair, seemingly braided so it would not move, responded in a sinuous way. She held in one hand the end of the single braid that usually fell across her breast.

"If I just do what he tells me to, or lets me do, what contribution will I make? Think of it, I might have run into him." She said this eagerly, as if she would have liked nothing better.

"Astrid, this man is a killer."

"I know."

"Then you better be careful."

"I'll be careful after he's caught."

"Then you won't have to be. None of us will. What were you doing in the hotel anyway?"

"I wanted to talk to the young woman, Mitzi Earl, about her experience with him. They wouldn't let me near her. Perhaps I could have used Richard's name and broken down their resistance. Instead, I sent a note up to her. If she got it, she didn't answer."

"She wouldn't see you?"

"Well, she didn't anyway. I don't know if the bellboy gave her my message. I should have followed him, though I don't know how I could. I was on the balcony, waiting to be paged, when it must have happened. Joanne, I didn't even know it had happened until later."

Joanne marveled at how seriously Astrid took this new project. She had never before spoken of her writing but now the library had her books and Joanne had read and been impressed by them. The book about the probable Viking descent into Minnesota after traversing the Great Lakes centuries before the Irish monks, let alone Columbus, came to America was fascinating. The chief piece of evidence was a stone found near Kensington, Minnesota, on which, among other things, the Hail Mary was engraved in runic characters.

"You obviously did on-site research."

"Yes."

"Who is Lars?"

Astrid sat back, surprised, but then began to nod her head. "The dedication."

"To Lars, with love."

"He was my husband."

"Johansen is your maiden name?"

Astrid laughed. "The next thing I know you'll be asking me to give one of your author talks."

"Would you?"

"Sometime, maybe. Certainly not now. My hands are full."

In the little bio on the dust jacket of the Kensington Rune stone book there was mention of a son as well. It was a moment when Astrid could have confided in her, told her important things about herself, what had happened to her marriage, what had happened to her son. Joanne was hurt deeply by her friend's silence. I expect too much, she told herself. I assumed that she felt toward me as I do toward her. But Astrid was more self-sufficient by far. If there were things missing in her life, if everything had not gone as she must have wished, she seemed ready to accept that and go on from there.

A support group had been formed since Richard Moriarity had talked at the library and its members tried to take comfort from the fact that the killer had moved into the city. The attack on Mitzi Earl on Walton Street in the city had suggested that the killer was moving eastward.

"That killing is different," Astrid said. "Having failed he tried again and succeeded. That took planning. The assumption about serial killers is that each murder is done almost on a whim, the victim a stranger."

"I'll bet if one of the first three escaped he would have gone back a second time."

"Maybe."

Joanne had the impression that Astrid was developing lines of argument for her book and was not willing to change her mind that easily.

Together they watched the televised arrival of Cecilia Vespertina. Afterward Astrid just looked at Joanne for a moment and then said, "I wish the woman no harm, but don't you wonder why killers don't go for someone like that rather than sweet and decent women?"

"She'll be signing books at the library for two hours the day after tomorrow."

"Signing library books?"

"We have a huge shipment of her books. They'll be on sale at the time."

"Selling books in a library? I thought libraries were for readers who can't afford to buy books."

"Progress."

They parted in the mall, since they had parked in different places. When Joanne had gotten her car and was coming around to the exit, she saw Astrid getting into a car that had a man at the wheel. On the spur of the moment,

Joanne pulled into a parking place so she could look back. The car was coming along the road just behind her, heading for the exit. Astrid was seated sideways in the passenger seat talking to the young man at the wheel, a young man whose features bore a strong resemblance to her own. Eric, the son?

Joanne thought less of herself for spying but largely because doing so had made clear to her how little Astrid chose to tell her about herself. Joanne had had no notion that Astrid had any friends or relatives in Schaumburg and now it appeared her own son lived here and she had never even mentioned it.

13

Katherine had called Walton Street several times but each time she found that Sister Mary Teresa was in chapel. She certainly did not want to bother her at prayer, if indeed she even could have done so successfully. Ginger Federstein did answer her phone and suggested Katherine go by the Palmer House with her.

"What does a death by strangulation do to one of Chicago's premier hotels? Catchy?"

"You underdo yourself."

"I'll think about that on the way past your place. I'll have the cab stop there."

The ghoulish side of her profession was impossible to defend, of course, and few journalists would try. The excuse for exploiting suffering and sensationalizing events was that everyone else did it. Why not then a summit at which a pact would be struck among all publications that certain things would no longer be done? Because immediately new publications would appear catering to the depraved popular taste. And of course the solid and respectable publications would have to compete with these putatively despicable rags.

"There is little logic in life, Katherine," Emtee Dempsey would say when they discussed this conundrum.

"I thought it was the other way around."

"That too. History is the great discipline. It takes things as they are, shapes them a little, but in the end it's Cleopatra's nose."

"What?"

"Pascal."

"Don't stop."

"Pascal said that the course of history would have been fundamentally different if Cleopatra's nose had been just a trifle longer. That is, if she had not exercised such a fatal attraction on Caesar and Marc Antony. History has reasons and causes but no logic."

Katherine, wearing a cape, a huge floppy tam-o'-shanter, and brandishing a cane, was on the curb waiting when Ginger's cab pulled up.

"I've decided you were flattering me," Ginger said, when Katherine had gotten in and arranged herself, taken a kiss on the cheek, and squeezed Ginger's hand with her own beringed one.

"Then I must have been."

"I could only underdo myself if my usual performance were high, right?"

"If you say so. But have you thought of another approach to this story?"

"Death comes to breakfast?"

"Ginger, without any doubt you have the demotic touch."

"You said that once before."

"Remarks are not Kleenex. They needn't be disposed of after one use."

"Demotic is not on my spell check."

She meant the dictionary stored in her computer. But Katherine refused to save Ginger a trip to an honest-to-God, bound and printed, massive dictionary.

At the Palmer House, they descended to the basement level to find Trunket the medical examiner conducting a press conference. For some reason the very bright lighting his technicians used while making photographs was still assembled and Trunket was strutting and fretting in its radiance while lofting lengthy answers to softball questions over the footlights.

"He'll get skin cancer if he doesn't watch out."

Ginger held Katherine back. It was the kind of scene that she as a columnist now eschewed, the difference between mere reportage and interpretation and commentary being everything to her now, although she had confided to Katherine that she now did with a good conscience what she had long done with a bad.

"I always told people how I felt about the news."

Katherine said nothing. Ginger was a friend and a valuable contact with the younger generation on the paper.

"You sound as though you'd been reading Cecilia Vespertina."

"Doesn't everyone?"

"That's a yes?" It was. Best not to react negatively to the enthusiasms of a generation that persisted in employing the categories of feeling everywhere. Was it possible to think contrary to one's feelings?

"Remember you're going to get me an exclusive with her."

"Remember? When did I say that?" •

"Won't you?"

"I'll see her in the morning." She could not resist the one-upmanship.

"You will! Where?"

"It's all very hush-hush."

"Let me come."

It might be a good idea to have Ginger there, Katherine thought. Emtee Dempsey would not object to her bringing a colleague and Cecilia Vespertina herself had never knowingly avoided publicity, she only wanted to control it.

It occurred to Katherine that here the two of them were

on the edges of a minor circus occasioned by the death of Mitzi Earl, whispering about the ring in the circus, yet it was here only hours ago that the life had been wrung out of Mitzi Earl. There are obscure deaths and there are deaths in the public domain but all deaths are quickly swept away by the living. Katherine raised her cane and quickly caught the attention of the medical examiner.

"Is Lieutenant Moriarity on the premises, Dr. Trunket?" she asked.

"I will be reporting to him as soon as I am through here and have had a chance to do a preliminary review of our findings."

The deference in his tone caused some in the press corps to turn around, a camera flash or two added momentarily to the glare from the tripod lights. Someone touched Katherine's sleeve and she turned to see Sergeant Gleason.

"He's still upstairs in eleven forty-one."

"Thank you, Phil."

As she and Katherine withdrew, Katherine saw Marv O'Connell, the inevitable complement of Gleason, standing unobtrusively some distance away. He nodded when Katherine flourished her cane.

They boarded elevators just down the hall and were whisked upward. It was gratifying to Katherine that her contacts were proving helpful. Stories of her insider connections would grow, radiating through the building from Ginger's office.

Room 1141 was a suite, richly appointed, temporarily turned into a command post by Richard. Members of his team from other jurisdictions had arrived and had been engaged in showing the composite of Oscar around to try to find witnesses of his presence there. One round-eyed waitress was talking to two detectives and seemed to be having mixed feelings about admitting to seeing a man who looked like the man in the picture she had been shown. It was dawning on her exactly who it was she had identified.

Richard nodded when she came in, but he was on the phone. Ginger immediately started to mingle, seeking the feelings she would later express in her column. Katherine, something teasing her memory, called Walton Street and Kim answered.

"Good, it's you. Katherine. What did you tell me about a scarf Mitzi Earl lost in the attack outside your door?"

She listened to Kim's confirmation that the scarf Mitzi had lost during the first attack seemed to be what she had been strangled with this morning.

"Cecilia Vespertina is coming," Kim said. "Tomorrow at ten."

"Did you see her on television?"

"She will more than meet her match tomorrow morning."

"You or Emtee Dempsey?"

Richard was putting down his phone so Katherine hurriedly said good-bye and passed on to Richard the fact about the scarf.

"I guess I assumed she was wearing it this morning."

"With that outfit?"

"You sound like Trunket."

"In what way?"

"He said she had no color sense, wearing that scarf with that dress."

"Pay attention to that man. I saw him downstairs in his portable tanning parlor instructing the press."

Richard and his team were engaged in the undramatic effort to link a particular man with the murder of Mitzi Earl. The problem was that, while they had reason to think Oscar had been here, or at least the man from the composite portrait resulting from the first attack on Mitzi, the fact that she simply had been strangled on the spot, and that the killer had disappeared, seemed to sever a link with the three murders they were engaged in investigating.

"We may be on a false spoor, so far as our job goes. It

looks as if we've got the same guy on Walton Street and here in the Palmer House. But is he the guy who was operating in the western suburbs? So far, out there, we have no one who is sure our picture matches anyone they have ever seen before. We don't have even potential witnesses on those three murders because we don't know where the girls were abducted."

Trunket, for all his showboating, ran a tight ship and what they were gathering—from the carpet, from the elevators he might have used, even the handrail on the stairway leading down to the restaurant—a basket full of long shots, might eventually tie in with something else that would enable them both to find their man and convince a prosecutor they had a case.

"Who is that woman?" Katherine asked, indicating a large but fit woman with braided hair of a color that momentarily defied Katherine's descriptive abilities.

"My collaborator." Astrid Johansen, who had persuaded Richard to write a book about the search of the serial killer.

"The Quest for Oscar?" Katherine asked.

"Hey, I like that. Maybe we can use it."

"Maybe indeed . . . "

"Isn't it yours?"

"The question is, can it be yours?"

"Geez, we authors are picky. Come meet Astrid."

14

The basic logistical problem next morning was whether they were going to get Monsignor McCarthy away from the breakfast table before the guests arrived at Walton Street. With a rubicund face, rimless glasses, silver white hair that looked as if he combed it with his fingers, he sat in street clothes, the newspaper laid out like a missal to his left, a heaping dish of scrambled eggs and bacon before him, sipping coffee as some sip wine.

"I knew housekeepers like you, Sister Joyce. But that was long ago. Women resent cooking for the clergy now, did you know that? Half the pastors in Chicago prepare their own meals."

Joyce fielded his compliments with deference. Monsignor McCarthy was seventy-seven, said their Mass each morning, and was at the end of a long and devoted priestly career. They considered it a privilege to have him. But it was very much of a good thing.

"Garrulity is the mark of age," Emtee Dempsey said tolerantly, then added, "One has so much to say." But then she escaped to her study and left entertaining the monsignor to Joyce and Kim, principally to Joyce.

"You spoil him," Kim said to Joyce. "No wonder he doesn't want to leave."

Joyce never complained about him. Now she had someone to discuss the sports news with. Like most Chicago fans, Monsignor McCarthy was a fatalist, expecting the worst. The Bulls? A fluke. A repeatable fluke, but no matter.

"Ataraxy, Sister," the old priest said. "It is the virtue of the Chicago sports fan."

"I never thought of it that way," Joyce said.

"You're being witty, Sister."

"I'm trying to figure out what ataraxy means."

"He who does not hope cannot be disappointed."

"Then why are we always disappointed?"

"Because we aren't virtuous," he said, like a Q.E.D.

From behind the monsignorial chair in the dining room, Kim caught Joyce's eye and tapped her watch. When she left, Joyce was asking the monsignor what time it was, her watch seemed to be running fast.

The monsignorial response drifted down the hall after her: "When you're having fun, Sister . . . "

It was after nine and the author of *Nine Ways to Self-Esteem* was due at ten, and they would not know until she got here whether she had already had her breakfast or not. Katherine would certainly arrive in advance of the guest of honor, and she was bringing a younger colleague with her. Margaret Mary was just coming up from the basement with an armful of folders.

"Can't you take your scanner down there, Mimi?" Kim asked.

"I'd have to take the computer too. I wouldn't want to work down there anyway."

"Of course not."

"Is the meeting between Emtee Dempsey and the visitor going to be private?"

"Private? It sounds like a seminar."

At Emtee Dempsey's suggestion, she had told Richard that his collaborator would be welcome. He liked the idea but he had called back to say that Astrid Johansen wouldn't be coming. Any disappointment Richard felt was masked by the remark that the author had no official connection to his investigation anyway.

"Can I sit in?" Mimi asked.

"Certainly you can."

Kim realized that she had begun to think of Margaret Mary simply as a technician, because of her prowess in computers. Their postulant was so docile and self-effacing it was easy to forget that she had been embarked on a very successful life in the world until things fell apart for her. That she was seeking to recover direction by testing her vocation to become one of their little community already suggested considerable character. Joining a large thriving community where she could have been lost in the crowd, so to speak, must have had its appeal, but she had chosen this anomalous remnant of an order trying to survive. Of course she could see in this remnant, thanks to her college memories, a good deal of promise. Kim had suggested that mature alumnae might be just the pool of possible postulants they were looking for.

Joyce made a face. "You already hear complaints about the graying of religious life."

"We could call it the delaying," Kim replied. "If we put them all in headdresses, who would know?"

The old nun had not said a definite no. It might seem to be an odd way to provide a future for the order, to rely on women whose religious life would be short by traditional standards. Mimi oddly showed little interest in the idea. But she would have an understandable inclination to see her situation as unique, not a pattern repeatable all over the place.

"Could you, when you get more data into the computer, check and see how many alumnae of your age are unmarried or widowed?" Kim asked Mimi.

"Sure." Mimi looked at Kim. "Is that why Sister wanted me to start with the last years and go backward?"

"Not everything she does has a reason," Kim said with a laugh. "But even her whims turn out to have benefits she didn't intend."

"Should I do such a survey?"

"Only if she asks you to. I'm still amazed at the prospects for the database. I suppose you could make lists of members of clubs, teams, that sort of thing, by the year?"

"Oh yes."

The question was not idle. Anne Webster had called to say that the airport interview with Cecilia Vespertina on Channel Nine had been seen nationwide and she had heard from a girl who had been in the Classics Club with her.

"It brought back such a rush of memories!" Anne cried. "We're in the yearbook and I have a scrapbook with clippings and photos, but without married names I wouldn't know how to get in touch."

"How did the other girl find you?"

"Oh, it's so good to be called a girl again! She knew my married name, since Greg and I were engaged my senior year."

Maybe they would be able to help Anne and other alumnae who wanted to reestablish friendships.

Katherine appeared at the door ten minutes before the hour. She looked back over her shoulder before stepping inside and doing a pirouette out of her cloak.

"Who is Monsignor McCarthy?" she asked Kim.

"Our new Mass priest."

"New! He's as old as I am. He stopped me on the walk and began to chatter and I couldn't get away."

"You know how old people are, Katherine."

The great eyes rolled to fix Kim with a stare. "By comparison with some, I am practically taciturn. Am I late?"

"You are first. In many ways."

"That's better." Katherine was still wrapped in an olfactory cloak of perfume as she swept down the hall to greet her old ally. She called over her shoulder, "Ginger seems to have forgotten, but if she shows up, let her in."

"Ginger?"

"Ginger."

"Roger."

Katherine stopped and her great eyes rolled once more at Kim before she disappeared into the study.

Telling herself that Katherine's colleague might have trouble finding the house, which of course was highly unlikely, Kim went out on the porch to keep an eye out for the young woman. No need to admit to herself that she was thinking of the dreadful thing that had happened to Mitzi Earl not many days before on that very sidewalk.

Soon a woman in a camel hair coat with long hair that caught the wind stepped from a cab, and did indeed look a little lost. She came toward Kim.

"Is this—"

"Are you Ginger?"

"Yes!"

"Katherine just arrived."

"She was supposed to wait for me."

Kim introduced herself and they shook hands. Ginger had hazel eyes and a wide, expressive mouth. She leaned toward Kim. "I'm dying to meet a nun."

"You just did."

She stepped back, grabbing at her coat that was just draped over her shoulders. "You?"

"Yes."

"I'll join. I love that dress."

"This old thing?"

"Don't say it's getting to be a habit."

"I can see why Katherine wanted you here."

Kim got Ginger inside and as she was pulling the door closed saw a great stretch limousine with dark opaque windows nose into the curb. Kim told Ginger where to put her coat and pointed down the hall. "Katherine's there."

The journalist had noticed the limousine too. "Don't worry. I'll get out of your way."

Fortunately, Mimi appeared to take Ginger off to the study and Kim prepared to greet the visiting celebrity.

It was the driver who came up to the door and asked if this was the Order of Martha and Mary, saying it as if he was ready to be laughed at. Maybe he thought he was part of a practical joke. Kim told him it was. He marched back to the car, stood beside it and looked up and down the walk. From a car parked ahead of the limo emerged two men Kim recognized as colleagues of Richard's, Gleason and O'Connell. A panel truck with a strange device atop it proved to be from Channel Nine and what must be print reporters poured from other cars. The driver opened the back door of his vehicle and stood at attention.

Emerging half crouched and then hurrying halfway to the stairs before assuming a fully erect posture was Cecilia Vespertina, actively ignoring the turmoil that rapidly developed in her wake. Her arms were away from her body, at eight twenty, and remained motionless as she glided up the stairs and across the porch to the door Kim held opened for her. She sailed inside, like Katherine in a cloud of scent, and Kim pulled the door shut and locked it.

"Well done!" the great lady said.

"I was about to tell you the same thing."

A dismissive flick of her hand, and then she devoted her full attention to Kim. Kim had never felt so *noticed* in her life.

"You are a nun?"

"Sister Kimberly."

The author seemed to be trying to find some deep significance in Kim's youth, her presentableness. Well, she was here to consider giving religious women her *placet*, as Emtee Dempsey called an affirmative vote.

"This way, Dr. Vespertina."

Of course there had been no question of their guest requiring identification. The others had moved into the living room and it was there that Kim led her. She felt a bit like the limousine driver when she went in ahead of her and announced, "Cecilia Vespertina."

It was, Kim would increasingly realize, a remarkable collection of women. The hostess, of course, Sister Mary Teresa, whose scholarly reputation had prompted the request for this meeting ("Now that I am in Chicago, Sister, I find that you are famous for other things as well"), Katherine Senski, as flamboyant as the visitor and, as Emtee Dempsey had said, a far better writer because she had a firm grasp on reality, and then Cecilia Vespertina. There was a warm if wary exchange of greetings, while Margaret Mary and Ginger Federstein, Joyce and Kim looked on.

"What a fascinating name," Emtee Dempsey said in a particular tone.

The celebrated author, enthroned in a brocade chair that matched the old nun's, laughed throatily. "In this setting, I will not pretend it is not a *nom de guerre*. But you would be surprised at how few people catch the allusion."

"A rather grim allusion, isn't it?"

"I felt much grimmer when I chose it. The object of my Sicilian Vespers was to be the male gender."

"Hardly a way to insure any future at all."

"That's it! But like many women, I was scarred by early experiences. I have grown out of bitterness, I hope, and now see the full appreciation of women as a condition of survival for the whole race. The elimination of men would, as you say, be apocalyptic."

They were off to a good start, one that was threatened when the old nun mentioned that she had met with Mitzi Earl in this very room. The author bowed in acknowledgment, but said nothing. Emtee Dempsey was not going to settle for that.

"In the short time she was in Chicago, she made a great impression on many of us. It is outrageous and appalling that she should have met a violent death here. I know that the police will not rest until they have found the man who did it."

"I will miss her very much," Cecilia said, but the remark had the note of a not quite grudging concession. As if to counter this, she added, "I shall not find her like again."

The preliminaries had included introducing all those in the room, of course, but even Katherine was more audience than participant in the discussion that followed. The author developed the remarks she had made at O'Hare when she mentioned her appointment to see Sister Mary Teresa.

"You mustn't think of nuns as a protest movement," Sister Mary Teresa warned. "The beguines, perhaps, but there have been ideologically motivated exaggerations in recent discussions of those women, who were not technically nuns. You perhaps know the concept of *contemptus mundi*?"

"I am a child, sitting at your feet," the author said.

Perhaps no remark was better calculated to bring out the excellent teacher Sister Mary Teresa had always been. In scarcely more than fifteen minutes, she put before the room a sketch of the history of religious women, beginning with the women who surrounded Jesus, going on to Jerome and then the great foundresses, Scholastica, Clare, and then the other medievals ("I will not sidetrack myself by bringing in Heloise," she said, and Cecilia cried out that then she must return to her later), and, so far as the Middle Ages went, recommending the work of her dear French colleague Regine Pernoud. The fate of religious women in the Reform and then into the modern era where, pardonably, Emtee Dempsey used Blessed Abigail Keineswegs as her model. Her peroration included encomia of the two American saints, Mother Cabrini and Mary Elizabeth Seton.

A short silence followed her presentation and suddenly

the room burst into applause. Emtee Dempsey, pleased as punch, brought it to an end.

"So you see, my dear, from its beginnings until now, religious life for women, the life of the three vows, has not been a life of protest, but an affirmation of eternal destiny and thus the pursuit of sanctity."

"And if I should substitute self-esteem for sanctity?"

Sister Mary Teresa rolled in her chair, making to those who knew her a supreme effort not to say what came immediately to her mind.

"It depends on what self is being esteemed."

"One's own. One's inner worth."

"But the women of whom we speak, and I am but the least among them, see the self as a gift, reflection on which leads inevitably to the giver. There is a loss of self in such self-esteem."

"That is too paradoxical for me and would be unintelligible to my readers."

Katherine intervened, having shown a heroic self-effacement, though she had hung on the old nun's words as much as anyone.

"What reader do you imagine when you write?"

The question obviously pleased the celebrated author. She pondered it a moment with closed eyes and without opening her eyes said, "Myself."

The pros and cons of this were gone into by the three quite different writers. Kim noticed that Margaret Mary was enjoying this enormously. She was so glad the postulant had been here for the historical sketch of the religious vocation for women, since she knew that Mimi, like any contemporary female, felt whipsawed between her natural inclinations and an incessant ideology that labeled them demeaning or worse. If any woman had to think her way through that thicket, she who would become a nun had a further task. Why forego the joy of following out those natural inclinations, a husband, children? Joyce on the other hand was getting restless. She had come expecting a brawl and this had turned into an intellectual gab-fest. She slipped away to the kitchen.

For her part, Kim felt the absence of Mitzi Earl. The advance woman would no doubt have been here for this occasion. Obviously Cecilia was on her best behavior, the martinet under wraps. Only her somewhat churlish reluctance to acknowledge the passing of her girl Friday had given an indication of the monumental ego that lay behind this celebrant of self-esteem. Her books were not nothing, certainly, but it was sad that readers had to settle for so shallow a vision of life.

Cecilia Vespertina was saying that she had been aware of the order's college from early on in her stay in this country. She had spent her first year in southern Minnesota ("My mother said that sounded like southern Alaska or southern Siberia") and often heard the college mentioned.

"We had students from Minnesota," Emtee Dempsey said. "Perhaps you met some of them."

"I forget the connection," Cecilia said, seemingly sorry she had brought it up. Did she sense a history of the college in the offing? "In any case, this has been a wonderful occasion. Can you give me a little reading list?"

"Of course. Where should Sister Kimberly send it?"

"She has been so quiet," Cecilia said.

"All ears."

"And very pretty ears."

"I expect Little Red Riding Hood any minute."

Cecilia gave her a card, they rose, and there were cordial good-byes. Cecilia looked on the verge of embracing Sister Mary Teresa but in time sensed that such contemporary fashions of affection were not smiled upon by the old nun. She had once surprised Joyce and Kim, illustrating her point about make-believe affection by reciting the lyrics of a once popular tune, "You Call Everybody Darlin'."

"I'll be expecting that list of books," Cecilia said on the

porch. She had marched to the steps and seemed to wait there for the groundlings to gather. Her driver stood ready at the door, Gleason and O'Connell were poised to run interference, she turned and gave Kim a little peck on the cheek, so much for theory, and swept down the stairs and across the sidewalk, this time acknowledging the presence of reporters, photographers, and passersby who had been intrigued by the stretch limousine and were now rewarded with a glimpse of celebrity.

Benjamin Rush was lunching at the Cliffdwellers with John Handy, the young man he had engaged as investment manager of the Order of Martha and Mary account since the death of his father. John Handy, Sr., had nursed a modest amount into a considerable endowment only to see most of it frittered away in the dissolution of the school and the loss of the vast majority of the nuns to more worldly pursuits.

Money was not a subject that engaged the deeper regions of Benjamin Rush's heart. He accepted the need for some few persons to devote themselves to the market, to its unintelligible fluctuations, to speculation in the stock of companies they would never see with an impact on the lives of employees they would never know. Long ago, in his youth, Rush had rebelled against this, expressing both his personal disinclination to engage in such activities and a moral judgment on the process itself. But entrepreneurial capitalism required capital; the market supplied the capital; unless one had another system that could fulfill this function on a national, even global, scale, protests were idle. Such was the mature view of Benjamin Rush. But he did not dislike any less the thought of concentrating on the medium of exchange.

The law might seem equally ephemeral to its critics, or to those not called to it, but for Benjamin Rush it drew its life and blood from the mass of the people and was nothing apart from the concrete actions that were enshrined in contracts, deeds, suits, and wills.

"The proposed sum is a million and a half," John Handy said, holding in his hand the speared olive he had just taken from his glass.

"Good heavens."

"It would be ours this afternoon, if I could in conscience make the asked for assurances."

This was far more interesting than an overview of the order's portfolio Benjamin Rush had assumed would ruin his lunch. Handy, besides being financial manager, was also what had once been called the fund-raiser for the order. The proposed gift was from a man named McFarland in Iowa. He wanted to endow the study of the classics and call the endowment after his late wife Susan.

"She attended the college."

"Apparently he hasn't heard it is no more," Benjamin replied.

"No, he knows that."

"Where does he suppose this study of the classics is going to take place?"

"He wants an assurance that efforts will be made for the order once more to operate a college. The endowment, he suggests, could operate as seed money, used to attract more, the better to realize the intention of going back into the business of higher education."

"Well," Benjamin Rush said, feeling an impulse he regarded as ignoble to promise the man whatever he wanted to get hold of that money.

"There is more. He would undertake to match other gifts to the eventual amount of ten million dollars. That includes the original million and a half."

"I hardly know what to say."

"Well, we're going to have to say something. I told him I would call him next Monday."

"I'm afraid you will be able to call him this afternoon."

"Ben, we are talking about a potential twenty million dollars."

"Which as you know in this day and age might get you a single building."

"Start small."

Benjamin Rush had to fight a tendency of old age to accept the triumph of the forces of evil, which in the present case meant that he, like Katherine Senski and, he supposed, even Sister Mary Teresa herself, had learned to luxuriate in their defeat of some years back. The lights were going out all over the world, nothing was as it had been, even darker times lay ahead. As a young man, he would not have understood the temptation to take pleasure in such lugubrious thoughts. But it was a powerful temptation and, he saw now, he had succumbed to it again and again. Hope came hard now, but he had no right to quash this magnificent possibility.

"You say his name is McFarland, and his wife was Susan. What was her maiden name?"

"He wants that in the title. The Susan Dowd McFarland Center for the Classics."

Benjamin made a note. "I will take it up with Sister Mary Teresa as soon as possible."

"Terrific. Now about those municipal bonds for the expansion of the sewage plant in Cairo."

"Egypt?"

"Illinois."

"Kay-ro."

At that moment their lunches arrived, Benjamin Rush's Monte Cristo sandwich, swimming in syrup. He said to the waiter, "Ask the chef if this is Karo syrup."

The best jokes are private. John Handy pretended he

had not heard, the waiter looked as if he wished he hadn't.

If Sister Mary Teresa felt any of the *delectatio morosa* that had affected him when John Handy told him of the proposed gift to the order, she did not show it. On the contrary, she rose from behind her desk, arms extended, eyes upraised and cried, *"Deo gratias."*

"Of course the proposal is founded on an impossibility," said Benjamin Rush.

The old nun sank back into her seat behind the huge orderly desk, but her expression of jubilation remained intact.

"The offer is predicated on your undertaking to promise that the order intends to take up again its mission to higher education."

The great headdress dipped forward, then recovered, as Sister Mary Teresa nodded. "That is why my joy is so great. This is the miracle for which we have been praying since we were driven into this redoubt. This has been Dunkirk, now at last a flotilla is on its way, eventual reconquest of the continent lies in the inevitable future."

"I can understand the attractions of such optimism, Sister, but is it realistic? You must give promises that are more than mere velleities."

"And so I shall."

"With three nuns, only one with the doctorate, and another a doctoral candidate . . . "

"I do not imagine that we could staff it with members of the order as once we did."

"But that makes it more unrealistic. Faculty salaries have risen dramatically since the college closed."

"But it is a buyer's market. There are idealistic, and unemployed, young scholars who would leap at the chance to take part in this great experiment in restoration."

Obviously her reaction was not a passing moment of madness. Once that became clear, Benjamin Rush set aside his own doubts and put his mind to the task of implementing Sister Mary Teresa's wishes. During the next hour, talk focused on the immediate formation of the Susan Dowd McFarland Center for the Study of the Classics. Sister Mary Teresa would talk with Vecchio at the Newberry about possible collaboration, she herself would lay out a program for the study of the transmission of the classics to the Middle Ages, thus playing from her own scholarly strength.

"Agnes DiLauria," the old nun burst out.

"Who is she?"

"You knew her as Sister Mary Benedict. She was one of the casualties of the great shake-up."

"And one of your major adversaries."

"We have been in touch of late. As shadows lengthen, one does not wish to carry on pointlessly old battles. Agnes thought she had won. Now she has profound misgivings about her role in the debacle. She has asked to be reinstated."

"And you will do it?"

The great headdress swayed negatively. "No. Reconciliation has its limits. But this McFarland offer permits a compromise. Sister Mary Benedict, as she was, holds a doctorate in classics from Toronto."

And thus the great castle was constructed in the learned air of Sister Mary Teresa's study. Agnes DiLauria might be named administrative director of the center, Sister Mary Teresa acting as president. Benjamin Rush would meet with McFarland and draw up a specific proposal.

"The thing to emphasize is that around this center, the pearl of a new college is to form. Benjamin, will we live to see the day when we purchase our old property and see restored what was so thoughtlessly destroyed?"

Sister Kimberly came in with the information the old

nun had asked her to gather, with the assistance of Margaret Mary's computer. The nun laid it on her desk but was too elated to appreciate Mimi's data on the study of classics at the college during the last quarter century of its existence.

On the assumption that Benjamin Rush might be dining with them, Joyce prepared veal marsala, to be preceded by artichokes and spaghetti alla bolognesa, with spumoni for desert.

"A typical Irish meal," she told Kim, who was doubtful they would be having guests.

"Did you know Benjie had been writing to Emtee Dempsey?"

"That came as a complete surprise."

"What do you think?"

"I've given up thinking for Lent."

"But it's not Lent."

"That proves I've begun."

The trouble with living with Emtee Dempsey was that they all started speaking with forked tongues. Mimi came into the kitchen with closed eyes, head back, distended nostrils.

"Now I'm sure I have a vocation. What smells so good?"

"I'll tell you while you make the salad," Joyce said. "*Insalata mista,* that is. We're celebrating Columbus Day."

"But that's in October."

"Well, he made a big mistake himself. This isn't the Indies."

"Will I become witty if I stay?"

"Nitwitty is more like it," Kim said. "What was the research project you were on?"

"Classics at the college in the last twenty-five years."

"What about it?"

"Everything. I put together the members of the department, the majors, officers of the classics club, winners of the annual prizes, notices in *Mmmm & Mmmm*, the student paper."

"Those of us in the Italian club called it the Mama Mia."

"And there was the short-lived Horace Club."

"Anne Webster!"

"She belonged to that. What a memory you have, Kim."

As she continued to prepare the special dinner, Joyce came to see she had a better memory than that for which she gave herself credit. It was the visit of the Websters to talk about their daughter that was the original prod, and now Mimi's mention of the Horace Club. And then another piece fell into place. She turned to Mimi, who was halving cherry tomatoes.

"Susan Dowd belonged to that group too."

"You're amazing."

Maybe, but when Joyce had everything under control and Mimi there to help besides, Kim went in to talk with Sister Mary Teresa and discovered the old nun was way ahead of her. She handed Kim a page of the printout Mimi had prepared. It was a list of the members of the Horace Club the year it was disbanded. Another item Mimi had found brought it all back. One of the girls had committed suicide after being expelled from the college on a charge of plagiarism.

"This is why I hate history," Kim said.

"Whatever for?"

"In the normal course of events, memories fade, sores heal, you forget. But this brings it all back again, fresh and awful."

There had never before been a suicide in the student body, and it could be argued that, since Sonja Hansen took her life after being expelled, the record was unblemished. But the girl had acted as she had because of her expulsion, so the school was inextricably involved.

"I have prayed for her every day since it happened," Sister Mary Teresa said. "It is not history but the communion of saints that keeps the past alive. What is Joyce cooking?"

Kim gave the menu but before she could explain that Joyce had presumed Benjamin Rush would be dining with them, the old nun clapped her hands. "What a splendid way to celebrate the feast of St. Eusebius of Vercelli."

Joyce, when told this, displayed her hands, hunched her shoulders in a Neapolitan manner, and said, *"Bé."*

A kid who worked in an ice cream store in Barrington thought he had seen the man whose picture had been constructed on the basis of Mitzi Earl's look at her assailant. Richard got out there as fast as the westbound interstate allowed in the late afternoon. Miscelli, the local captain, had asked the kid to come down and put it on the record.

His name was Russ, he had hair so long he wore it in a net at work. He was a mouth breather, and he had brought both his mother and a cousin who was a lawyer with him.

"Russ will proceed only if we get an ironclad promise there will be no publicity."

Beamer, the lawyer cousin, looked as if he specialized in non-negotiable proposals. Richard just sat in a corner, following the proceedings, if there were going to be any. Russ had said he recognized Oscar but that had been off the record and if he backed away now, there was nothing they could do about it. The mother wore slacks and heels and was wringing her hands. Given Oscar's record, it was hard to blame them for an onslaught of caution.

"No problem," Miscelli said.

"I want it in writing," Russ demanded.

"You write what you want and I'll sign it."

"But will you mean it?"

"With a piece of paper like that you could sue the department into the Stone Age if we made an announcement."

"I said *any* publicity."

"Russ, have you told anyone else about this?"

The kid looked at his cousin as if he would know. "I told my mom."

"Your mom we can trust," Beamer said.

"Anybody else?"

Russ had told two other kids who worked in 43 Flavors.

"Shall we say the point is moot?" Miscelli asked Beamer. "Chances are it will be in the papers in no time."

"Russ, that was dumb," Beamer told his client. The mother told him to watch his tongue.

"Russ," Miscelli said warmly. "I want to tell you that the citizens of the greater Chicago area are going to thank God that you had the guts to step forward and give us the first tangible piece of evidence. The store 43 Flavors is in the Winger Mall, isn't it? That's where Irma Walsh had gone to pick up a film she'd had developed? She picked it up and was never seen again. You know where the photo store is?"

"Next door to us."

"You're what we've been praying for, Russ. I want you to meet Lieutenant Richard Moriarity, of the Chicago police. He's director of the special task force. You've read about it, you've read about him. I called him and he flew out here to talk with you."

Russ's mother liked this approach.

The kid's testimony put Oscar close to where Irma Walsh had last been seen, next door in the ice cream store, to be exact. After Miscelli got it down and over Beamer's objections got Russ to sign it, the Barrington chief couldn't avoid glancing at Richard. This was hard stuff at last, a living witness. Richard had turned on his tape recorder as soon as he had arrived. They now went out to the mall, in

Richard's unmarked car, Russ, Miscelli, and Richard, with Beamer and Mom following in the cousin's car. The idea was to be as unobtrusive as possible.

Remaining in the car, they looked at the photo store and the adjacent ice cream store. Somewhere in this parking lot two lines had vectored and joined, Irma Walsh coming out of the photo shop, Oscar from the ice cream store. They were parked more or less where Irma Walsh's car had been found, presumably where she had parked it. The abduction could have taken place within feet of where they now were.

"We ought to get a psychic out here," Miscelli said.

"What?" Richard was astounded.

"A psychic, you know. Someone with powers. That's what they did in the John Wayne Gacy case. This woman came to a place, closed her eyes, and told them what had happened there. It turned out later, she was right."

"We know what happened here."

"Yeah."

Judy, another clerk in 43 Flavors, said she had been meaning to come forward, but she was scared, but now that Russ had talked she would too.

"The picture makes him seem older than he is," she said. "He'd been in here before."

"You saw him more than once?"

Her jaw moved with the gum she was chewing. She nodded. "I thought he was going to make a move on me. You know?"

If girls could stand the sight of Russ, maybe Judy wasn't as ugly as she seemed. She wore black—black T-shirt, black tight slacks, high black shoes. A sleeveless black sweater completed her outfit.

"He ever talk to you?"

"He ordered a lemon sherbet cone."

Russ felt upstaged by this detail. He had never served Oscar, had never heard him speak, if only to order a lemon sherbet cone. Judy had usurped the spotlight, and Beamer objected.

"You're leading the witness," he said.

"I'm asking questions," Miscelli said.

"Leading questions."

"Who are you representing here anyway? Russ, is this guy your lawyer or what?"

Russ looked at his mom, who gave him no help. "He's my cousin."

Miscelli suggested that Beamer stop interfering with a police investigation.

"I'm an officer of the court."

"Then it would be a shame to have to arrest you."

Beamer conferred with Mom since Russ was as interested in what Judy said as Richard and Miscelli.

"Whyn't you say this before?"

She shrugged, she chewed her gum, she looked at Miscelli as if she thought *he* might want to make a move on her. Richard was finding her less persuasive than Russ. The other employee of 43 Flavors suddenly decided he had been mistaken in saying he recognized Oscar.

It was a shame Astrid was missing all this. Richard had left a message on her answering machine and half expected her to join him here, but that entailed that she had returned within the last hour and a half and listened to her messages.

It was decided that Miscelli would put all possible personnel on the task of taking that picture everywhere in the vicinity. If Judy had seen him several times at the ice cream store in the mall, it was even possible that he lived in Barrington. Meanwhile, Richard informed the rest of the team of the development, and suggested that departments contiguous with Barrington do what Barrington was doing with Oscar's picture.

Since he was close, Richard drove over to Schaumburg to the address Astrid had given him, a development of fairly expensive-looking condos. He got out of the car, slammed the door, turned, and found himself face-to-face with Oscar.

Richard stared at an Oscar younger looking than their composite picture of him. The shock of recognition immobilized Richard momentarily and Oscar too was frozen. Enough time seemed to pass for Richard to recite the Gettysburg Address if he could have remembered it and then he shouted.

"Hey!"

Why "hey" he didn't know, but it might have been the starter's gun. The kid took off like a gazelle, crossing the lawn, heading for the condos. It was youth against sedentary age, but Richard set off after him and for the first twenty-five yards he felt he could catch him, he would run him down, wear him out, but he was going to catch him.

Between two condos, over a hedge, into a field that had been scraped clean, prepped as a building site. That was when he felt the stitch in his side and realized that the roaring sound was his own breathing. Ahead of him, Oscar seemed to pick up speed. But he was heading for the interstate along which cars were moving swiftly and in large numbers. The interstate with its traffic was like a huge fence, hemming Oscar in. It gave Richard a second wind, and he jogged on, certain now he would trap his prey.

Oscar didn't even hesitate when he reached the interstate but ran right out into traffic. Richard stopped, unbelieving, expecting at any moment to see Oscar crushed by one of the speeding vehicles, or tossed into the air as by a charging bull. Horns split the air, there was the screech of brakes, a car came bumping off the road, through the shoulder, and then flipped, describing a high lazy circle, before it hit the ground with a dull thud. On the road there was the crashing sound of cars smashing into other cars. A great semi, its cab jackknifed, slid through a mass of cars like a bowling ball. There was total chaos.

And then on the far side, still running, he saw Oscar.

God knows how much damage he had caused, how many injuries, even deaths, but there he was loping away, free as the breeze.

"I'll get you," Richard said aloud. "I'll get you."

He went to the car that had landed on its roof. As he drew close, he saw that the roof was crushed down almost to the level of the window bottoms. A heart-rending screaming emerged from the wreckage. Richard got a grip on the handle and tried to open the door, trying to avoid looking inside the car. But he did and his eyes met the person who was screaming in agony. He rose, turned away, and threw up. He could do nothing.

Sirens were screaming to the four winds. Richard waited until some paramedics hurried toward the overturned car, and then walked slowly back to where he had left his car, moving through the people who were being drawn to the scene. He alone knew what had happened. Motorists would no doubt tell of a crazy man who had run out into the interstate, but they wouldn't know who he was.

Richard sat behind the wheel of his car, trying to expunge memories of that overturned car from his imagination. It seemed to him now that he could have helped, he could have done something. That screaming person could be dead now. He wiped his mouth, checked his clothes, he seemed all right. It came almost as a surprise when he remembered that he was here because he had been going to drop in on Astrid.

He found the address and pushed the bell. Before he could push it again, the door opened.

"Richard, what a surprise. Come in."

As he walked through the door, he decided to say nothing about his chase and the pile up on the highway.

"Did you get my message?"

"Message?"

"On your answering machine."

"There wasn't one from you."

"There has to be. At the sound of the tone I told you to meet me at Barrington."

She went to the machine and punched the rewind, stopped it, and played the messages, some of them for Eric. Richard's message was not among them.

"I must have done something wrong."

"You can hear that the machine works."

"Who's Eric?"

She smiled. "My son."

"Oh."

"Why did you want me to meet you in Barrington?"

"Two witnesses saw Oscar in the mall on the night that Irma Walsh was abducted."

"In Barrington."

She sounded relieved that it wasn't in Schaumburg. It was the time to tell her that he had run into Oscar right outside this development and had chased him. . . .

But he didn't. He would, but not now. There was no need to worry her. Besides he did not want to tell her about the highway, the car that had flipped and landed it on its roof, and the agonizing scream of the crushed driver.

News of the multi-car crash on I-94 spread through the library, all but emptying it, even staff just took off to see what had happened. Joanne herself felt no desire to go. Looked at it from a distance, cars and trucks moving along it in stately parade, the interstate seemed harmless, but driving on it filled Joanne with terror. Jorge drove that road every day and Joanne didn't even want to think of how many near accidents he had going and coming. When the skyline of Chicago came into view to the east, something happened to otherwise sane drivers. Trucks roared along at twenty miles over the speed limit, passing one another, switching lanes with abandon, crowding out the cars, which in retaliation or just for the hell of it darted from lane to lane with little forewarning as the traffic hurtled toward O'Hare and, visible on the horizon, Chicago itself.

In her office she called Astrid to see if she had heard of the accident.

"When?"

"Minutes ago."

"The interstate?"

"That's what I'm told."

"Joanne, can I call you back?"

"Sure."

Without reason, Joanne felt rebuffed. Had she been making a pest of herself? From the beginning, she had placed too much importance on her friendship with Astrid. It was meant to make up for so many other things, deficiencies in her life, at work, at home too, in a way, though God knows she wasn't unhappy. She didn't want a different life than the one she had, she just wanted to feel more confident and content. It seemed weeks since she and Astrid had had one of the lengthy conversations that had characterized the first phase of their friendship. It was when she learned that Astrid had a child, a son, and not because Astrid told her, but because she had seen her with the boy, Eric, that she realized how reserved Astrid was. And there had been a husband too.

Why should that matter? Jorge had met Astrid, an introduction, little more, and Astrid had seen her kids, but it was as if their friendship existed independently of husband and family and all the usual things. Of course, Astrid was so much more accomplished than she was. . . .

No! She had to stop thinking that way. For heaven's sake, she was director of one of the most successful library systems in the western suburbs, the envy of her counterparts because she had money to do almost any plausible thing, she had a huge staff, community relations were excellent. Not only had she gotten Cecilia Vespertina to come, but it had been her idea to invite Richard Moriarity, and she had been able to do it because she could draw on her status as an alumna of Martha and Mary, Richard being the brother of one of the younger nuns living with Sister Mary Teresa on Walton Street in Chicago. Astrid had gone up to Richard after the talk and that was the genesis of their collaboration on a book about the serial killer. Joanne had been at least the midwife of that.

Joanne hadn't heard much about that book lately, but then she hadn't seen much of Astrid lately. Well, she would wait for Astrid to call her. It must appear to Astrid that she had little or nothing to do, despite her responsibilities, since she always had been ready to meet for coffee when Astrid suggested it. She had to stop expecting so much of everything and everyone.

What she needed, she decided, was a long talk with Sister Mary Teresa. Her hand went out to the phone, but she stopped it. No, she wouldn't make an appointment, she'd just stop by there tomorrow. The library ran like a watch whether she was in her office or not. With the drive into Chicago on her agenda for the next day, Joanne got ready to call it a day. She fussed around another ten minutes before finally leaving her office, and she knew why. She was hoping Astrid would call back.

As she went past the circulation counter, she said goodnight to Irene and then heard a phone ring. She'd transferred her calls to the counter before leaving her office and she slowed her pace. She stopped to look at a display devoted to Carl Sandburg. The phone had stopped ringing, someone had answered it. She waited to see if Irene would call out and say it was for her. After some moments, she looked back. Irene was busy checking out a book for a user.

After a minute spent staring at the simian face of the Chicago poet, Joanne continued on outside.

If she'd had any doubts about her reception on Walton Street, just dropping by as she did the following morning, they were quickly allayed.

"Mimi," Sister Joyce cried, taking Joanne's hand and leading her to a room where a woman was working at a computer. "Look who's here, Mimi. Joanne Heit."

The woman turned and Joanne recognized her immediately. "Mary Margaret! What are you doing here?"

Sister Kimberly came in and while Joanne was being told about Margaret Mary being a postulant, they moved on to Sister Mary Teresa's study, where the old nun took Joanne's hand in both of hers and just beamed at her.

"Another member of the Horace Club," she said.

"Is that all you remember about me?"

"Of course not. But it is just serendipitous that you should come by today."

Everyone seemed to talk at once, they insisted she stay for lunch and of course she agreed. Her grasp of what Mimi was doing with the computer, compiling a database of the college records, impressed Sister Mary Teresa.

"Sister, my library is high tech from one end to the other. Books are only a part of it."

"Did Richard Moriarity have a triumph there or is Sister Kimberly exaggerating?"

Joanne described the occasion in detail and they all hung on her words—the turnout, the questions, the proposal that he write a book on the investigation he was directing.

"Now if I could persuade you to come lecture, my life would be complete."

"Who would want to leave their television for an evening in order to listen to a superannuated nun talk medieval history?" Her pudgy little hand quieted the protests. "Richard's collaborator wrote an interesting book on the Kensington Rune stone, by the way. You might bring her by someday."

Joanne nodded, but she had the selfish thought that she wouldn't bring Astrid. She half feared that the nuns would be far more interested in Astrid than in herself.

At table, the topic was the Horace Club and, under the prompting of Margaret Mary, Joanne began to remember more and more of that short-lived effort. It had been disbanded her junior year. Why was that? And just as she was about to ask, she remembered.

"Sonja Hansen."

Margaret Mary nodded. After all these years, the two women looked at one another with a shared guilt. It was the first death Joanne had known, of someone close, someone she knew, and because of the kind of death it was, she had asked herself what she could have done to prevent it. But that meant preventing the thing that led to Sonja's expulsion. Sister Mary Teresa was saying that the long ago occurrence showed the fecundity of evil.

"One evil brings about another, or disposes for its coming about. We treated her unjustly, that is the nub of the matter."

"What was it she did?" Joyce asked.

"Plagiarism." Mimi spoke in almost a whisper.

"That was the charge," Emtee Dempsey said. "I never believed it for a moment. Something far worse than plagiarism had happened and Sonja was innocent."

"Wasn't it proved, Sister?" Joanne asked.

"Oh to a faretheewell. There was evidence galore. That's why I knew something was wrong. I counseled delay, at least, but it was felt that an example should be made. Of course plagiarism, like other academic cheating, makes a mockery of the whole educational enterprise, grades become empty ciphers, one pretends to know rather than knows. It is a very serious matter indeed. But it is far more important to be certain the charge is true."

Recalling all that took some of the glow off her visit, but the talk turned to other things. Emtee Dempsey, with great mysteriousness, said that a very exciting announcement would be made in a few days.

"The answer to my most fervent prayers."

On that promising note, the meal ended. Joanne had a few minutes alone with Mimi and again promised her whatever help she could be.

"My computer person is a whiz," Joanne confided.

"This is really a very simple project. Huge, but simple."

"It's kind of scary though, isn't it, having all of it at your fingertips? I had forgotten all about Sonja. Isn't that awful?"

"What if Emtee Dempsey is right and she didn't even do anything wrong?"

Joanne took secondary roads back to Schaumburg, as she always did. When she pulled into her reserved parking space, she was in a far better mood than when she had pulled out of it. On a bulletin board just inside the entrance the composite picture of the serial killer was prominently posted. Joanne went by it, then retraced her steps and looked again at the picture. She wouldn't have said it aloud for the world, but that picture could have been Astrid's son Eric if the suspect had been a boy instead of a man.

There was a message saying that Astrid had returned her call, but Joanne got the busy signal when she tried to reach her. She kept trying, without success, and found it impossible to forget it. At four o'clock, having gotten the busy signal for an hour and a half, she left and went by Astrid's condo. What she expected to see she didn't know, but when she got to the corner, she made a U-turn and pulled into Astrid's driveway.

The blinds were pulled, a rolled newspaper lay in front of the door. Tonight's? It was too early for that. The house looked as if Astrid were away, yet the phone had been busy. Joanne got out of her car and closed the door hard, making a loud noise. As she approached the door, she heard music coming from inside, loud as could be, and not at all the sort of music she associated with Astrid. She rang the bell but wondered if it could be heard over the racket of that music. The building seemed to pulse with it. The neighbors must be going beserk. If the phone hadn't been answered, she could almost believe that the ringing had been unable to compete with the music. But the phone had been busy.

She went around the building and found that the screen door was ajar and the inner door was open. She cupped her hands and called through the screen.

"Astrid, are you there?"

She slowly pulled open the screen door and stepped into the kitchen, again calling out Astrid's name. That dreadful music seemed to push at her, almost forcing her outside again. Acting as she would have if it was one of her kids playing music that loud, Joanne walked through the kitchen and into the living room where she found the switch of the stereo and plunged the room into blessed silence.

The phone was off the hook. No wonder. Then her eyes were drawn to the floor.

Astrid lay there, twisted, bloody, her long braid trailing from her smashed head, her eyes wide open but seeing nothing.

Kim had feared Emtee Dempsey was going to mention the McFarland gift and the further prospect it opened up, but she had used the knowledge only to tease Joanne. Mr. Rush and John Handy were coming by later, after Emtee Dempsey's nap, to discuss a draft of the legal aspects of the proposed center. Agnes DiLauria would be in to see Sister in the morning.

All the exciting good news Benjamin Rush had brought was a tonic for the old nun. Before leaving, their lawyer had taken Kim aside.

"Katherine Senski called you about my concern?"

"Yes."

"Had she advanced this imaginative hypothesis to you?"

Kim had been if possible more upset by Emtee Dempsey's off-the-wall hypothesis that the serial killer currently plaguing the Chicago area would be found to be motivated by hatred of the Order of Martha and Mary. At least that seemed to be what she had implied. Kim had sought to reassure Katherine when she needed reassurance herself. But she was far more confident in answering Benjamin Rush. There hadn't been another mention of the fanciful explanation. Of course Emtee Dempsey had said there wouldn't be. Now she had all this good news to turn her mind into more profitable channels. And her mind had never seemed sharper or more focused.

Kim knew everything that was happening, the unexpected bonanza from Mr. McFarland to commemorate his late wife, an alumna of Martha and Mary, the sum usable as a matching grant that could rise to ten million dollars, thus making twenty million dollars a realistic objective. These were simply facts, true as facts are true, but was it really possible that after the lapse of more than a decade the college could rise from its own ashes?

Of course it wouldn't be exactly as it had been. It would be a semblance of the college in the way that the three, now four, of them in the house on Walton Street were a semblance of a once-flourishing order of teaching nuns. A topic she and Joyce had always avoided was what would happen after Sister Mary Teresa was gone. But the topic hadn't avoided them. The cardinal conveyed to Emtee Dempsey that, if the order was simply fading away, attracting no new vocations, canonical provisions would have to be made for its dissolution. There was, of course, money and property involved. The communication, delicately phrased, deliberately avoiding any note of menace, had sent a chill through Kim. So many nuns had left the convent in recent years. Would the convent now leave her?

Now suddenly, unexpectedly, from a quarter no one would have suspected, new hope had been born. The money came at a moment when at last they had a postulant and what the money would enable them to get under way would bring the order to the attention of young women who could be attracted to the life it offered them. If only Kim could believe that would come true.

She was called from the meeting with Benjamin Rush and John Handy that had been going on in Emtee Dempsey's study. The phone call, Joyce said, her expression significant, was important. In the hall, after she had shut the study door, she turned impatiently to Joyce, but her expression stopped any expression of impatience.

"Joanne."

She might be calling to thank them for the lunch, but if that's all it was, Joyce would not have called her from a meeting, its subject upon which their future depended. She went into the kitchen and picked up the phone.

"Sister Kimberly."

"Has Richard told you the news?" Joanne asked.

"What news?"

"Oh, Sister, it's awful. My friend Astrid Johansen is dead. Murdered. In her home. I found her!"

The voice rose through stages to near hysteria. Astrid Johansen was the author who had persuaded Richard to collaborate on a book concerning the serial killer.

"You called Richard."

She had called Richard, yes, but not from the house. She couldn't use that phone. She didn't even hang it up, couldn't touch it, just left it hanging there the way it was and ran outside again. Apparently she had run about on the front lawn, crying and calling out for help until she had roused the neighborhood. The police came and she talked to them and that's when she thought to call Richard.

Kim gave such consolation as she could over the phone. What a terrible shock it must have been to call on a friend and find her like that. There was so much Kim wanted to ask, yet did not want to ask Joanne in her state of mind.

"Are you home now, Joanne?"

"Yes, I'm here. At home."

"And who's with you?"

"The boys are here, and Stella. I'm waiting for Jorge."

"Then you're not alone."

"Oh, no no. I'm with my family. Sister?"

"Yes."

"I kept thinking of Sonja."

Joanne's husband came home while she was on the line and Kim felt better about cutting off the conversation. She put down the phone and turned. Joyce stood immobile in the middle of the kitchen, waiting. What had she made of half the conversation?

"Is there any coffee?"

Joyce darted to the cupboard for a mug, then filled it and brought it to Kim, keeping her eyes on her throughout.

"Astrid Johansen is dead. Murdered. Joanne found her."

"Was it Oscar?"

"Oscar?" The serial killer. "My God, I never thought of that. But this was in her home."

Joyce nodded. "He killed Mitzi Earl in the Palmer House."

"I can't tell Emtee Dempsey, not now, and I can't rejoin the meeting as if this call didn't come."

"Had you ever met Astrid?"

Why did she feel so personally hit by this? Joanne's jumbled grief had been contagious perhaps, but there was something ominous here that Kim did not understand, something that would affect them all. . . . She shook her head, stopping herself.

"I'm getting as bad as you know who."

"In what way?"

"I'll explain later. Or I'll try."

And she got up and went down the hall to the study and rejoined the meeting that would affect the future of the order.

20

Richard talked with the officers who had answered the call the neighbors had made, reporting the crazy woman who was running around screaming and crying. At first he thought they meant Astrid, that the neighbors had complained about the noise she was making and then she went inside and got killed. He found it difficult to just shut up and listen and find out what happened. This was bad.

He was in the yard where Joanne Mendoza from the library had been running around, discussing the scene with those members of his task force that could make it there.

"Was she sexually assaulted?"

"The coroner says raped."

"Anything else?"

"Why don't we wait for his report?"

"How'd he get in the house?"

"The Mendoza woman found the back door open."

"So we know how he got out. The front door was locked, right?"

"For days."

"Why do you say that?"

"Yesterday's paper was out there. Mail still in the box."

Schwartz came back from the house. "No sign the back door was forced that I can see."

Odds and ends, bits and pieces. Richard thought of the last time he was here. He thought of encountering Oscar and chasing him to the interstate. He hadn't told her. He hadn't wanted to frighten her. The serial killer was running around her neighborhood and he hadn't wanted to frighten her with the information. Schwartz remembered that Richard had thought he spotted their man when he came to talk with Astrid.

Richard could see that they were all acting casual. To them, he was a big shot from Chicago dropping in on a Viking princess in the suburbs, his "collaborator" on a book. Richard knew what he would think if any of them had such a story. No wonder no one would look him in the eye. He wanted to explain it to them, go on about it, but that would have been fatal. He could only hope their wonderment about him would not harm their common investigation. At the moment I would not want to be working for me, he told himself. I sound like a hot dog who is up to no good with some woman I was letting making a pest of herself, and now she's dead just days after my last visit when I let Oscar get away, trying to outrace him when what I should have done was get in my car and sound the alarm.

"Let's go inside," he said aloud.

Nothing had been done to the body. Richard forced himself to inspect it, to crouch beside her and see her as he would see any other corpse in the line of work. He remembered throwing up after he had seen the inside of that car the other day. He stood up and moved back. My God, this was no time to burn out. He was going to catch the man who had done this!

"What's wrong here?" he asked his group.

The looked around, thoughtful, but it was not a question they were likely to answer. He told them.

"Oscar is the guy who killed three women in the western suburbs. He abducted them, raped, killed, mutilated them, then dumped them in obscure places. Weeks, months, went by before they were discovered."

"This one would have been hard to handle," one investigator said. "She was big."

"With a knife at her throat, she could be handled. He chose to kill her here. That's two."

"Mitzi Earl."

"Right. We got two abductions and two on-site killings, The one in the hotel is a comparatively clean job. He just choked the life out of her."

"But he had tried to snatch her earlier."

"Yeah. So only this one clearly escapes the pattern."

"But he did improvise," Schwartz pointed out. "When he failed with Mitzi Earl the first time, he just tried again and killed her."

"And why did he have to kill her?"

"She had seen him."

"But if he killed this woman, Astrid, because she saw him, why not *just* kill her. Why rape?"

"He had her in her house. It wasn't the corridor of a hotel."

And a house could be covered in a way a hotel corridor could not. Richard wanted the technicians to do a job like they'd never done before. Still, it was a mixed case. Oscar did not fit the emerging pattern of the serial killer, a mark of which was repetition, the same deed in the same way over and over, as if the sameness of what was done introduced some pale imitation of rationality into a brutally irrational activity.

Before breaking up, after this brisk and cooperative exchange, Richard decided to address the latent uneasiness of his team.

"Let me say a personal word here, more or less personal.

As you know, the deceased approached me with the proposal to write a book on our investigation after I spoke here in Schaumburg about the case. She had written books, and I only write checks, when I'm lucky, and reports. We had a verbal agreement, a formal agreement was being prepared. We never got to that point. But the idea was that we would proceed as if we had that agreement. Some differences had arisen as to what she could and could not do. On her own, she tried to get an interview with Mitzi Earl, when we had Mitzi under tight security at the Palmer House. Astrid tried to finagle her way past police security. Obviously, she had no clearance from me to do that. We had words about it. On other occasions, when I wanted her to be at what I thought would be an important element in any book, she refused or failed to show. Now she's dead. Oscar had been in this neighborhood. I know, I saw him. I thought I could run him down. I was wrong. What I never expected was that he would run across I-94 in heavy traffic and make it. He wrought havoc for lots of others; there were three deaths and God knows how many injuries. He's still out there. This woman is dead."

"Do you think she had made contact with him?" Schwartz asked.

"I don't know. It never entered my mind. But that's a smart question."

"Do you think the book idea was a blind?"

"That's another thought I didn't have."

"So it's okay if we go ahead as if maybe she isn't just a victim?"

"Yes."

That he hadn't even raised such questions in his own mind despite the things Astrid had done and not done told him that the collaboration had been a bad idea from the beginning. Maybe it was just what it seemed, maybe her agent was just a slowpoke who hadn't gotten around to the agreement yet, maybe Astrid had just been enterprising when she pulled the stunt she had at the Palmer House. Maybe.

But there were other possibilities and one that seemed painfully obvious now was that she had bewitched him with the book idea, and all the money he would make from it, in order to insinuate herself into the investigation. The Palmer House incident made it clear that she would act on her own without letting him know what she was up to.

"There's one other thing," Schwartz said, looking Richard straight in the eye.

"Yes?"

"Where were you when this happened?"

Miscelli started to laugh but then didn't when Richard glared at him.

"That's the best question yet. I've opened myself up to it because of this supposed collaboration, a collaboration which as I've just said wasn't going according to plan. It's hard to fit this into the MO of Oscar, not impossible but hard. So maybe I've had a real falling out with Astrid. I feel I've been had. Some good-looking woman has talked me out of my shoes. So what do I do? I report seeing Oscar in the neighborhood. I make use of the multi-car crash on I-94 brought about according to motorists by some idiot sprinting across the lanes. I say that was Oscar. I've set it up. I come out here, have a showdown, we have a fight, I hit her, she falls, hits her head, whatever. In a panic, or out of cold planning, I make it look like Oscar has been here."

He sensed as he spoke that consciously or unconsciously some such scenario as this had been lurking in the backs of their minds.

"Where was I? At a hearing where we disciplined the three officers who had been standing guard at the Palmer House."

That irony cleared the air definitively and Richard felt that he had resumed moral command of the team. They broke up but Schwartz stayed behind.

"Not many people would have been as frank as that, Richard. Or as self-critical."

"This is an awful way for it to end, but I should never have considered such a collaboration. At least, not until our job is done. It was a stupid move."

Schwartz didn't disagree.

"Now we can get going interviewing the neighbors."

Back to the routine. The technical people would turn the house inside out for leads, detectives would interrogate neighbors, fanning out from the house like circles expanding on water, in the remote hope that someone would have seen something that would give them a lead.

What turned up was an abandoned four-wheeler that had been in the parking lot of a little business center not far from Astrid's condo. The dry cleaning people had thought it was someone at the take-out pizza store and vice versa. After a couple days, they had their doubts but didn't act on it.

"It's not unusual for businesses, usually restaurants, to have a few cars in the lot," one of the pizza guys said. "Then people won't be put off by the thought that no one else is inside."

Asked if anything whatever unusual had happened in recent days, strangers, whatever, the dry cleaning man had pointed to the four-wheeler.

"How long you say?"

"Yesterday? It's been overnight at least once."

In the pizza shop, a delivery driver had noticed when the vehicle was first parked.

"I been wanting us to get something like that. You get rammed at some intersection in that thing, you might survive."

"It would roll."

"With those roll bars who cares?" He had the manic look of a formula-one driver.

The detective checked out the vehicle visually then, instinctively deciding not to disturb any prints, dirt, whatever. He radioed in.

Some of the air went out of it when the vehicle turned out to be stolen.

"Where?" Richard asked.

"Barrington."

The four-wheeler was taken away for examination and the owner, initially elated that his vehicle had been found, now began to raise hell. Richard explained to him the importance of what they were doing and of the owner keeping quiet.

"You mean that killer stole my vehicle?"

"We don't know that. But it's possible."

He decided to keep quiet. "When you're done with it, I'll sell the sonofabitch."

Maybe he would get a lot more now than he figured if he did. There were people attracted to such ghoulish items. Oscar might have doubled or tripled the value of that four-wheeler in the curiosity market.

21

I f good can come out of evil, one welcome result of the death of Astrid Johansen, thought Katherine Senski, was that it should shake Sister Mary Teresa from the absurd theory she had proposed, both to Katherine and to Benjamin Rush, to the consternation of them both. How on earth their dear old friend could have imagined a connection between random killings in the western suburbs and the Order of Martha and Mary was a question best left unexamined. The slightest reflection on it had led Benjamin Rush to wonder if they were witnessing the decay of a great mind.

"Not a word since we spoke of it," Benjamin assured her. "This McFarland gift has proved a real tonic for her."

"A million and a half dollars! Some tonic. I'll take that with my vodka any time."

Rush and John Handy had met with Sister Mary Teresa the previous day, at the meeting from which Kimberly had been called to receive from the hysterical Joanne Mendoza the news of the slaying of Astrid Johansen. It was a horror from which Katherine expected the indirect good result that Sister Mary Teresa would treat with benign neglect her own fanciful theory. Katherine was thus reassured by Benjamin Rush's statement that there had been no further speculation along these lines.

This morning, Katherine would go to the house on Walton Street for a meeting of a far more delicate kind. Sister Mary Teresa would be interviewing Agnes DiLauria, the former Sister Mary Benedict. Informed of this last night by telephone, Katherine had been thunderstruck.

"Sister Mary Benedict! She is your mortal enemy. Don't tell me you have forgotten."

"Forgotten, no. Forgiven, I hope. Have you said the Lord's Prayer today, Katherine?"

"You can forgive her without welcoming her into your nest."

"She will not be reinstated in the order. Even if I were agreeable, I doubt that Rome would agree, and it would have to go to Rome. She left with a certain panache."

Had she not. Interviewed on television—was it "Kup's Show"?—she had declared a unilateral renunciation of her vows. She had not been coerced into taking them in a physical sense, she admitted, but she claimed that there had been severe psychological pressure once she entered the novitiate to accept her vocation.

"A begging of the question, needless to say," the woman who already styled herself Agnes DiLauria said, looking shrewdly at the camera. "But such constraints and repressions have been thrown aside by the council. Windows have been opened to let in fresh air. My vocation, the only vocation any of us has, to love one another, can best be served as Agnes DiLauria, not as Sister Mary Benedict."

Such statements still had news value in those days. For a day or two, Agnes was propelled from channel to channel, from talk show host to talk show host, the newspapers reporting her increasingly bitter statements about the order. That caused sadness to some, but to others it was a clarion call. Thus it was that one of the leaders in altering the mission of the order, which had led to the selling of the college, now led the departure of many from it. The proceeds from the sale of the land and buildings were distributed among members of the order—including former members—as back payment of wages due.

This was the woman Sister Mary Teresa proposed meeting with in her study on Walton Street in a house that would have been auctioned off with everything else if Benjamin Rush had not stood athwart that road to ultimate ruin.

"You will remember that she was professor of classics, with Latin as her specialty."

"I remember many things about her."

"The McFarland bequest envisions the formation of the Center for Classical Studies. I think Agnes is ideal for administrative director."

"At her age?"

"I had not expected you to manifest ageism, Katherine," the old nun said with ill-concealed relish. "Besides, she is younger than you and I."

"Combined?"

"Now, Katherine."

"I am opposed."

"When the college is born again you will of course be a member of the board. Then, your opposition will be more than an expression of personal opinion, duly registered."

Regardless, Katherine had promised to be there at ten. She arrived at nine thirty, when Agnes was still closeted with Emtee Dempsey and Katherine could sound out the younger nuns on this preposterous proposal.

Joyce said, "I wonder how many of those who couldn't wait to get out of the convent and hit the beaches have had misgivings since."

"I haven't heard of any."

"They wouldn't get the audience their statements of rejection did."

"Maybe the word should go out, subtly, that they are welcome back. Not to full status. I don't imagine they themselves would think that right. But there could be an association with the order."

"Nonsense," Katherine said. Was she to be the last to keep a level head on her shoulders? "Most of them are married, more or less."

There was of course no way of proving or disproving that there was a pool of potential penitents out there, eager to come home after years of wandering. But Katherine thought, and said, that it was an insult to those nuns who had remained faithful to expect them to welcome back women who had pilloried and mocked the life they themselves had led steadily through the years.

"Remember the prodigal son, Katherine."

She rose from the table, nearly upsetting her coffee cup. "Son. That's the point. Men are different from women, more head than heart, but women give themselves completely to a thing, they identify with it far more totally. They cannot just swing back and forth the way men can. There are no stories of prodigal daughters."

She fled the room as other biblical stories began to be cited, women at wells, women caught in adultery. Honestly, sometimes Katherine thought that the greatest danger to Christianity was Christianity.

"And how are you doing?" she demanded of Margaret Mary, looking into what they were calling the computer room.

"What are they talking about in the kitchen?"

"The prodigal daughter."

"Me?"

The woman's eyes widened as she asked and Katherine, devastated that she should have made Margaret Mary think the others thought of her as a castaway, hurried across the room and gathered her into her arms.

"No, my dear. About me."

She stepped back and asked Margaret Mary to tell her all about what she was doing.

"At the moment I am organizing data into a report for Sister Mary Teresa. There was a Horace Club at the college, just ten girls. I was a member myself. It was disbanded in our junior year—"

"Sonja Hansen."

"So Sister has told you of it."

"I remember the incident. It had a profound effect on the morale of the college. I have sometimes thought that the expulsion of that girl was the beginning of the fissure that eventually led to the ruin of the college."

"I can tell you that those of us who were members of the club were hard hit by it."

"What was the relation between the club and the charge of plagiarism?"

"It was the translation of the famous Ode 38, Book One. You know, 'Persicos odi, puer, apparatus . . . ' We all worked on it together, it really belonged to none of us, but Susan Dowd probably had most influence on the final result. It appeared in *Poetry* magazine under Sonja Hansen's name."

How quaint the world had been so short a time ago. Would such an incident even raise an eyebrow today? After all, Sonja had had *something* to do with the translation. There were many ways in which its attribution to her alone could have been explained.

"Are there minutes of the inquiry?"

"Yes. In Latin."

"Latin!"

"Sister Mary Benedict was secretary of the committee appointed to hear the case. Keeping the record in Latin was partly affectation, partly a matter of confidentiality."

"But then all the testimony is in effect her translation, not the words actually spoken."

"I never thought of it that way. But she was a marvelous Latinist."

Kim looked in. "You're being summoned, Katherine."

"Are you coming in?"

Margaret Mary shook her head. "I haven't been asked."

So this would be a meeting of the ancients. Agnes Di-

Lauria, Katherine was happy to see when she entered the study, had not aged well. It would have been difficult to specify the color of her hair, her jawline was all but gone in a general crumbling of flesh, her eyes were set in deep shadowy pockets, but her manner indicated that all this external ruin was hidden from her. She rose in majestic confidence.

"Katherine."

After a moment's hesitation, Katherine put out her hand and Agnes, surprised, took it. That small victory put Katherine at ease.

"Margaret Mary has just been bringing me up to date on the Horace Club."

"Agnes and I have been discussing the same thing."

"You were faculty moderator, weren't you?"

Katherine was about to call her Sister but succeeded in not doing so. She had never called her Agnes, and did not see how she ever could. She resented the ease with which Emtee Dempsey visited with this Judas Iscariot.

"I was. For years now I have felt responsible for the events which led to the closing of the club."

"You were insistent that Sonja Hansen be expelled, as I recall."

"How certain I was of everything in those days. Except of important things."

Katherine was not sure she could abide a repentant Agnes DiLauria. Katherine had had her share of colleagues who finally acknowledged that they were alcoholics and made a breast-beating career out of not drinking. The therapy seemed to involve boring everyone else to death with the story of one's degradation. Now former smokers threatened to put even these professional penitents in the shade, mounting moralistic crusades against the habit that had once afforded them consolation, blaming others for the pleasure they had taken in it.

"You think it was a mistake?"

"I have proposed to Agnes that a preliminary step to the setting up of the Center for Classical Studies might be a reunion of the surviving members. These women might have valuable suggestions—two went on to do graduate work in classics. Perhaps more financial support might come in this way. Margaret Mary's database bears out how well our alumnae did in a worldly way. Bringing all that up to date is a necessity. And of course the reunion could be a pleasant way of welcoming Agnes back."

"So that's been decided?" Katherine asked.

"Katherine," Agnes said, turning to her with a sorrowful expression. "I know you find it incredible that I should be thought of for such a post as this. I myself can hardly believe it."

"The prodigal daughter?"

"Exactly! Then you do understand. Can you accept me back, Katherine?"

"I'd be a poor Christian if I couldn't."

Agnes came to her and put her arms about her and kissed her cheek. As the lips touched her cheek, Katherine was looking directly at Sister Mary Teresa whose mouth formed a bow of a smile, but the light had rendered the lenses of her glasses opaque. Katherine patted Agnes's arms. Perhaps the outward display of forgiveness would change her inner attitude in time.

"A certain amount of emotion is appropriate at a time like this," Emtee Dempsey said when Agnes was once more seated and dabbing at her eyes. "But we must not become maudlin. Back to the proposed reunion."

During these past difficult years, several alumnae had sponsored reunions, bringing classmates and husbands together in a Loop hotel. Emtee Dempsey attended, of course, speaking with great effect and much wit to her girls, but she had found such experiences ambiguous, telling Katherine they seemed like get-togethers of survivors of the sinking of the *Titanic*.

"Were there any?"

"Look it up. But you must see my point. It is painful to have our girls think of their college as something that was and is no more."

"At least they are thinking of it."

The reunion of the Horace Club, considered as the harbinger of the resurrection of the college, elicited unequivocal enthusiasm from Emtee Dempsey.

Katherine did not stay for lunch, unwilling to put her newfound virtue to further test. She realized, as she hailed a cab, that her visit had not been purely ceremonial. Emtee Dempsey had wanted and received her *placet* to this extraordinary new development in the fortunes of the Order of Martha and Mary.

"Her mind is clear as a bell," she told herself. But then she added, "The Liberty Bell." The driver's eyes appeared in the mirror, curious about the old lady in back, talking and laughing to herself.

22

Wasn't she a friend of yours?" May Wilson in acquisitions asked Joanne.

"Yes."

"Extra copies of her books are on order."

"She would have liked that."

Later when May Wilson realized that Joanne had discovered the body, she was no longer as considerate as she had been. It must have seemed odd that Joanne wouldn't have mentioned something as important as that.

Joanne found that she no longer cared what her subordinates thought of her. Astrid's death cast a long shadow over the ordinary concerns of life and now Joanne easily rose above what had been causing her so much pain and concern. She felt released to the self that had been before her elevation to the directorship, knowledgeable, efficient, reliable. For the first time she brought these characteristics to her performance as director.

And she could confront the fact that Astrid had deceived her without becoming upset. What she had hoped would be a special and undying friendship, now looked to have been a calculated using of Joanne, principally to make contact with Richard Moriarity. Once Astrid had gotten his agreement to a book collaboration, Joanne had served her purpose. It seemed odd to her now that she hadn't realized that before. It would have saved her much anguish if she had.

But all that was behind her now. She felt a new cynicism possess her and it had the effect of making it easier to get along with people. No longer really trusting anyone, she found it easy to work with them, staying on the alert for the moment when they would turn on her. Given this new lucidity about Astrid, she was unprepared for Richard Moriarity's interpretation.

"It was a con game, I think. She talked written agreement and contract and big advances, but nothing emerged."

"But don't those things take time?"

"It was supposed to be rush-rush, take advantage of the idea while it was hot."

He hadn't come to talk with her about Astrid, at least not in this way, but once he started he went on. He thought she intended to write a book, but not with him.

"She tried to bribe her way past police security to interview Mitzi Earl at the Palmer House."

"Maybe she didn't want to put you on the spot by having you open all the doors for her."

He looked at her kindly. "Well, you're a loyal friend, at any rate."

"Astrid was in many ways a secretive person. She didn't confide in me, not really."

"I thought you were close."

"She had a son and I didn't even know it. One day I saw her with him and asked and she said, oh, that's Eric."

"There were pictures of him in the house."

Joanne didn't want to think of the house. "I never met him."

"But you saw him."

"Yes."

"Would you be able to recognize him?"

"Recognize him? What for?"

"Could you?"

What an odd question. She told him no, she hadn't seen him that clearly, simply that it was a young man driving the car, and that had surprised her and when she asked, Astrid said it was her son.

"Did he live with her?"

"I don't know. Haven't you talked to him? Good Lord, doesn't he know what happened to her?"

"He hasn't shown up."

"Really?"

"He seems to have a room in the house, but he hasn't come back."

"Oh my God, I hope nothing's happened to him."

A few days ago she had envied Astrid and wanted desperately to be her friend so that some of that grace and confidence would rub off on her, but now Astrid was dead and her son apparently didn't even know it. That she had envied someone who had only days to live, whose family had fractured, whose son could not be found, made her want to weep.

"She had a husband too, you know. They were divorced."

"He the boy's father?"

"I assume so."

"Look, you apparently knew her better than anyone and you don't seem to know much about her."

"That's not my fault."

"I'm not blaming you. But she turns out to be a real mystery woman. I've contacted the editors who published her books but the latest one came out ten years ago, and she hadn't been in touch with them."

"Where had she lived when she was in touch with them?"

"Minnesota."

"She wrote a book about a Viking stone found in Minnesota."

Joanne had hoped that this book would be the real bridge between them, given her own background in classics. Once she had read Virgil and Cicero, even Horace, with ease. She had been part of an elite at college, all classics majors, or at least minors, and they formed a club, the Horace Club. They were subjected to the usual undergraduate wit, called the Neighsayers in the student paper, greeted with "Et tu, beauty" and asked what Horace's handicap was. And they loved it. It was fun being just the ten of them. Until the awful thing about Sonja Jensen and her expulsion and suicide and then they all lost heart in it and dissolved the club.

Astrid hadn't even wanted to hear the story, saying she couldn't bear to think about suicide.

Richard Moriarity said, "I have the feeling you're holding something back."

"I'm not."

He pulled at his lower lip and looked around her office. "I blame myself."

"You do?"

"The other day I came to talk to her about our supposed collaboration and when I got out of the car I turned and found myself looking into the face of Oscar. He could see I knew who he was, and he took off. I took off after him. That was stupid."

"It's your job."

"My job is to apprehend criminals, not challenge them to a track meet. He was half my age. When he outran me and I came back I didn't tell Astrid I'd seen him."

"Oh."

"He made an attempt on Mitzi Earl that failed, and came back again. Whatever he was doing there, I had interrupted his plans. Well, he just postponed them."

"You think he was there to kill Astrid when you saw him."

"It looks like it."

"What would she have done if you'd told her? She was a pretty gutsy woman. When she wanted to interview Mitzi Earl, she just went down to the Palmer House and tried to get in to talk with her."

"You think she would have stayed around?"

"Of course she would have."

"Maybe you're right."

"Well, then."

"My reason will seem crazy. Do you want to hear it?"

"Of course."

"When I faced Oscar I knew who he was, but I could see Mitzi hadn't gotten him right. She made him look older than he was. He was a kid in his twenties."

"You think Astrid wouldn't have left her house because she figured she could handle someone that young."

"Something like that."

"What then?"

He let some moments go by, as if he were not sure he would say it, but then he did.

"I think Oscar is her son. I think Oscar is Eric."

23

Joanne obviously thought he was crazy and maybe he was, but he had hoped that laying it on her like that would shake her up. There was a reticence about her that Richard had not been able to break through, and he had a hunch that she thought what he did but she didn't want to acknowledge it. If it was fear, he could understand that, but that didn't seem to be it.

So it was a disappointing visit, but the investigation now seemed to be a series of disappointments, since they expected their inquiries to lead nowhere.

"He's out there somewhere," Schwartz said. "He knows we're looking for him and he's laughing at us."

One of the kids in the ice cream parlor had talked to the wrong person and the newspapers were full of the big breakthrough in the search for Oscar. Witnesses had been found.

Beamer called and accused Richard of breaking a solemn agreement.

"Yeah, I remember when I signed it."

"It doesn't have to be written down to be binding. There were witnesses to it."

"Beamer, I've got the whole thing on tape. If you'd like, I'll send you a copy. You were told that the police would not make public your nephew's name or that he had seen the killer near where Irma Walsh was last seen. That promise was kept. We did not promise that your nephew would be smart enough to keep his mouth shut."

"Now wait a minute."

"Your time's up."

He slammed down the phone. If anyone had a complaint it was the girl who worked in the ice cream store. She was a more likely target than Russ. He made a point of this to Schwartz.

"We start losing witnesses to this maniac and the press will be all over us."

Media accounts suggested that Richard was deploying several regiments of cops, fanning over the greater Chicago area, omnipresent, omniscient, within days of finding their man.

Several times he had been on the verge of saying what he thought about Eric Johansen, but he held back. An effort was being made to find the slain woman's son, it wasn't as if he were being ignored, but he wasn't being looked for as a suspect. Trying it out on Joanne Mendoza had been a fizzle. It was time to gamble that he was right.

He convened his team at a Bennington's, let the others do the talking, reporting on the non-results of what they had done.

"Every time we seem to get something solid, it turns out to be not much," said one detective.

"True, but so what?" said another. "He was seen in the mall the night Irma Walsh disappeared. He killed someone in broad daylight in the Palmer House."

The usual complaints. Schwartz sensed that the media was getting impatient. They had overplayed the ice cream store witnesses and were likely to blame the task force because it hadn't led to a rapid arrest.

Coffee came and Richard sat forward. The others had

been conscious that he hadn't said much, and they wanted to hear him now.

"I think I know who he is."

Total silence. It was as if someone in the wings had turned up the sounds of the other diners and they were in a little island of stunned silence.

"I think I know who it is because I faced him. He ran and I went after him."

Schwartz said, "You told us that. All you're saying is Oscar is Oscar."

"No. I'm saying Oscar is Eric Johansen. The kid I faced was her son. That came to me when I was in the house and saw pictures of the kid I had chased. They are pictures of her son Eric."

"But she was sexually assaulted."

"That's why I've held back on this. The guy's a monster, but even monsters have limits. My guess is this guy doesn't. Or he did what he did to the body to take suspicion away from himself."

"But he knows you know him."

"That's why we can't find him. A woman is killed and we can't locate the son who apparently lived with her."

"We're dancing as fast as we can."

"I'm going to get us help. From the media."

He called Katherine Senski, not being able to think of anyone he'd rather give a scoop to.

"Do you have pictures of him?"

"Do you want them delivered to the *Trib* or to your office?"

"Send them to Ginger Federstein at the *Trib*. I'll be there when they arrive. What about television?"

"A press release will be given out in an hour."

"So what's special for me?"

"You get an exclusive interview with the director of the task force."

"When?"

"I'll meet you at Ginger's office."

The interview with Katherine enabled him to take a fresh look at the investigation. Recent events emerged with more or less clarity.

- Three abductions of young women had taken place in different western suburbs, over the span of half a year; they had produced a cumulative effect and a recognition that they were probably the work of the same man—a man who could slip easily between the cracks because of the different police jurisdictions involved. The formation of a task force, with Richard Moriarity in charge, was a clear indication that there would be a full-court press to apprehend the killer before he struck again.

- Responding to a request from the director of the Schaumburg library, Richard laid out the present state of knowledge about serial killers, making it clear what a formidable task they faced. After that talk, he had been approached by Astrid Johansen, a writer, proposing that they collaborate on a book devoted to the investigation currently under way. A verbal agreement was struck, to be swiftly followed by a written agreement between Richard and Astrid Johansen and then a contract with a publisher. The prospect of large profits was emphasized.

- Mitzi Earl, in town to prepare the way for her employer, the celebrity self-help author, Cecilia Vespertina, was attacked as she left the house on Walton Street where Sister Mary Teresa Dempsey resided. Vespertina wanted to interview the nun in support of her contention that religious women were forerunners of the women's movement. Mitzi warded off the attack, thanks to gymnastic agility, and was able to help construct a portrait of her attacker, presumably Oscar, the name assigned to the unknown killer.

• An around-the-clock three-man guard was assigned to Mitzi Earl at the Palmer House. Nonetheless, she returned alone to the restaurant where she had breakfast to retrieve the purse she had left there. She was attacked and killed in the basement concourse, the murder weapon the scarf that was taken from her in the attack on Walton Street.

• Astrid Johansen, without the knowledge or permission of the police, was at the Palmer House, attempting to interview Mitzi Earl, presumably for the planned book. She unsuccessfully bribed a bellboy to deliver a note. The bellboy says he flushed it down a toilet. If he is lying and the note was delivered, that might have been what brought Mitzi to the basement.

• Routine inquiries with the picture of the killer, produce first one, then three, witnesses of the presence of Oscar where one of the three victims was last seen and on the night she was last seen.

• The man who attacked Mitzi Earl on Walton Street and the man who strangled her in the Palmer House were the same man, the link being Mitzi's scarf. The picture based on Mitzi's look at her attacker produces an identification in Barrington, so there is a basis for concluding that it is the same man involved in all these incidents.

• Richard Moriarity grew increasingly unhappy with his supposed collaborator Astrid Johansen. She shows up where she shouldn't (Palmer House) and refuses to show where he suggests, the house on Walton Street for the big all-female powwow with Cecilia Vespertina. Furthermore, no progress has been made toward a written agreement between them, let alone a contract with a publisher. He drives to her condo from interview with Russ the ice cream store clerk and when he gets out of his car, turns and finds himself facing Oscar. Oscar takes off, Richard pursues, with an incredible multi-car pile up on I-94 caused by Oscar's sprinting across the lanes of the interstate, throwing motorists into a panic trying to avoid him.

• If Richard had gotten back into his car and made the report he should have made instead of running after the suspect. . . . He returned to talk to Astrid, who assured him the formal agreement between them was being written up, and he did not tell her that he had seen Oscar in the neighborhood. Why this omission? He did not want to frighten her. He got a first intimation of the identity of Oscar when he noticed photographs of Astrid's son in the house after her murder. He was withholding information until their collaboration was clarified. None of these reasons was defensible.

• Astrid Johansen was found murdered in her house. The condition of the body points to Oscar, but since Astrid is Oscar's mother if Oscar is Eric, Richard hesitates. Would Oscar attack his own mother and in this savagely brutal way? Overcoming his scruples on this score, Richard Moriarity today announces that Eric Johansen is the primary suspect in five recent murders in the Chicago area, including that of his mother.

This was the account that emerged from the interview with Katherine—rather, the elements of the dramatic account that would appear under her byline in the next edition of the *Tribune*. Maps were supplied. The picture constructed with Mitzi Earl's help was balanced on the other side of the page with a photograph of Eric taken from his mother's house. The picture of Richard looked like his high school graduation photograph.

"You should have your picture taken more often," Kim said, when he stopped by Walton Street.

Emtee Dempsey was frowning over the story, which she had already read in the typed version Katherine had faxed to the house, a fax machine being another item in the so-called computer room Margaret Mary had put together.

"The story suggests that the three original killings were random, Richard," the old nun said.

"That is one of the marks of the serial killer. He selects his victims without apparent rhyme or reason. They aren't persons for him, women with names, families, friends, and all the rest. One woman is as good as another for his purposes. Oh, there may be subjective requirements on his part. The victims of a serial killer look uncannily alike."

"And that is the case here?"

"You could argue it either way."

"They don't appear very similar in these photographs."

"That's true."

"The profile of the serial killer seems to be a Procrustean bed into which you are forcing all your facts."

"Procrustean bed?" Richard repeated, looking around for help.

Agnes DiLauria explained the reference. If the occupant was too big for the bed of Procrustes, his feet protruding from the end, say, he was cut down to size; too small, and he was stretched on a rack. Thus, one bed fitted all.

"Well, they're all dead," Richard said. "That is the similarity that interests me."

"And you're confident that you know who the killer is."

"I'd bet this house on it."

"No, you will not. Richard, you may succeed in capturing this killer, but proceeding as you are, you will miss the large point."

"Which is?"

"Why he did it. His motive."

Richard was tempted to read the old nun a graphic lecture on those first three killings and that of Astrid Johansen. In the antiseptic air of the house on Walton Street, it was difficult to imagine the condition of the bodies of the victims. Seasoned homicide men became sick when they viewed the victims in the condition in which they were discovered. Sister Mary Teresa could look at the little postage stamp–size pictures of those young women and say they didn't appear similar to her. But their deaths had been similar; the assault, the mutilation, were the same. Motive? Richard tried to explain that this guy just wanted to produce more corpses like those. The old nun simply didn't understand that they were dealing with an evil, demonic force and it made little sense to ask why precisely these three women rather than three others. In this context the question simply did not arise.

"An excellent job," Sister Mary Teresa said suddenly. "Excellent."

Finally she was giving a little credit to him and his colleagues. Richard was about to make a self-deprecating remark that might spur her into further praise, when she added, "Katherine is a marvelous writer."

24

nto the enthusiasm and euphoria of clients, it was Benjamin Rush's duty to introduce caution and circumspection. This did not make him the life of the party, as one might say, but the legal mind seeks not to amuse nor to egg on to bemusement so much as to call to attention, to be a voice of sobriety in a gathering of inebriates and emphasize that ever ancient, ever new truth that there is no free lunch.

The McFarland gift was a bonanza in the present condition of the Order of Martha and Mary, there was no doubt about it, and the celebration of that fact as such would find Benjamin Rush's uncertain baritone added to the chorus. The further prospect of twenty million dollars to be achieved by matching the McFarland gift as it rose to ten million dollars was, while hypothetical, a thought with its feet on the ground, and Benjamin Rush would toast it as Cardinal Newman toasted the Pope.

It was when, from these two launching pads, wild talk began of the reopening of the college, buying back the land and getting the same old buildings again, walking the very lawns of yesteryear, that Benjamin Rush was inclined to remove the stars from the sisters' eyes and restore them to the sky where they belonged.

So when he heard his dear friends and clients talk of a public confession of the college's error in expelling Sonja Hansen as the center piece of the announcement establishing the McFarland-sponsored Center of Classical Studies, Benjamin Rush, catching the scent of litigation, felt compelled to counsel no, no, no, a thousand times no.

"It is simple justice, Benjamin," Sister Mary Teresa said.

Basil McFarland, who had flown in for the meeting, a lean and hungry-looking jogger whose concept of health was a cadaverous physique, said Susan had often expressed regret about what had happened to Sonja Hansen.

"I don't know how many monasteries she signed her up for perpetual masses in," he said.

"A holy and wholesome thought," Benjamin conceded. "I am not opposing such recompense, if recompense there should be. What I fear is a suit for damages which would not only wipe out Mr. McFarland's generosity but might also jeopardize the property the order retained after the closing of the college."

"But who would sue us?" Katherine Senski asked.

"Presumably the dead girl has relatives. Has anyone looked into that?"

Sister Mary Teresa nodded to Margaret Mary. "I haven't yet entered all the records of that class into my database, but I did look at the physical records," the postulant reported. "Her application for admission is there and her financial aid statement, so we could find what relatives she had when she matriculated."

"Make that part of your other project, dear," Sister Mary Teresa said.

"That would be helpful," Benjamin Rush conceded. "Thank you. I also wonder precisely on what this collective *mea culpa* is based. It is at once understandable and commendable that the members of the Horace Club should remember their former classmate and regret the tragic circumstances of her death. But I detect here the acceptance as a fact that the girl was indeed innocent."

"I would testify to that," Agnes DiLauria said quietly. "And I was the principal proponent of her expulsion at the time."

"I understand you were the secretary of the committee that made the inquiry."

"Yes."

"Are those notes intact?" His question brought titters of laughter from Margaret Mary, Kim, and Joyce.

"They're in Latin, Mr. Rush."

"Were the proceedings conducted in that language?"

The laughter became general. Benjamin Rush looked brightly about, unused to eliciting such a response. When the merriment ceased and he pursued the question, he made the obvious point.

"If the proceedings were recorded in a language other than the language of the inquiry, a question could be raised as to their status as records."

"Oh, Benjamin, that's nonsense," Katherine said. "Court records are kept in shorthand, are they not?"

"Which is a version of the actual language used, as the written language is a sign of the spoken language."

"Well, the Latin records are a sign of the English spoken at the inquiry."

"That is not the same thing, Katherine."

"Why are we discussing this?" McFarland wanted to know.

Benjamin Rush was happy to spell it out. In the event of a court case, of the order's being sued by surviving relatives of Sonja Hansen for defamation of character, which arguably led to her suicide, the defense would have to produce the records of the decision to expel. The fact that the records were in Latin could lead a court to bar their admission. This could be tantamount to a directed judgment of guilty.

"Why don't we wait until Margaret Mary has completed her research?" Sister Mary Teresa suggested.

Benjamin Rush was content. He had introduced the note of caution and secured a lawyer's best friend, postponement and delay. That being done, he opened his briefcase and brought out the papers which would establish the Center of Classical Studies as an entity of the Order of Martha and Mary. He read out to the meeting the main points he had covered and was pleased enough to see eyes glaze over.

"The ideal of the end," he observed, "must yield to the realism of the means."

"Read on, Benjamin," Sister Mary Teresa said.

"And cursed be he who first cries 'Hold, enough,' " Katherine continued in a stage whisper.

The meeting ended on a single note, the establishment of the center. McFarland called his pilot to have the plane ready, using a phone from his briefcase, and then took Rush aside and congratulated him on his exposition. "When you talk, I can understand. Were they serious that committee notes were kept in Latin?"

"Apparently."

McFarland shook his head and rose on his toes. He looked about to engage in some quick exercise to burn off a few calories. Benjamin figured that with another twenty pounds, the entrepreneur might be a good-looking man.

"When Susan talked about the college and that club, I always thought of it as a sorority. That sort of thing. But it meant a lot to her."

"This center is a good idea."

He meant that it could be implemented, legally, financially, but he felt no need to pass on to the donor his doubts about its internal constitution. He intended to ask for a memorandum laying out the intentions for the first five years of the center. Without a clear plan for additional personnel, he was afraid the Illinois secretary of state would shoot it down.

"Why must it be registered separately as a not-for-profit corporation, Benjamin?"

Sister Mary Teresa was asking a friendly question. She had the layman's conviction that things could be done swiftly and informally and no bad results would follow. But if he had not formed the remnant of the Order of Martha and Mary into a new corporation and deeded over to it the concessions he wrung from the rebellious nuns, claims could be made on the house on Walton Street and the property in Michigan on behalf of the order as it had been. But the order as now legally constituted, while it might hire people for tasks related to its present work, was not in a position to invoke its tax-free status for such a thing as the Center for Classical Studies.

He did not, of course, ask that these things be understood. It was sufficient that he was given freedom of action to protect the sisters from possible results of their present enthusiasm.

"What is the 'other task' of Margaret Mary to which you referred, Sister?" Benjamin Rush asked.

"I knew when I said that you would pick up on it."

"In the context, I found it intriguing."

"It won't get us into any legal trouble, don't worry about that."

His initial curiosity was increasing as she spoke. "But you can tell me what it is."

"Just a little theory of mine."

Any contentment the meeting had given Benjamin Rush fled at these words. The gleam in those still youthful blue eyes behind her gold-encircled lenses was the one that had alarmed him earlier and about which he had consulted Katherine Senski. The hope that the excitement created by McFarland's generosity would have driven that fanciful theory from her headdress seemed unfounded.

"Is it a theory we have spoken of before?"

"And I agreed not to bring up again?"

So it was the former madness returned. The old nun laid a hand on his arm, said she must say a word to Mr. Mc-Farland before he flew away, and thumped across the room. Benjamin Rush went in search of Katherine Senski.

25

Kim, taken aside by Katherine and Mr. Rush, assured them that Sister Mary Teresa had said no more of her alarming theory that the recent serial killings in the Chicago area would find their explanation in the Order of Martha and Mary.

"I am afraid she has not forgotten, Sister Kimberly," Mr. Rush said in mournful tones. "She as much as admitted it to me just now."

"And I thought she was her old self again," Katherine cried.

"Her young self," Mr. Rush corrected. "The matter arose when I asked her about the other task Margaret Mary is engaged in."

"As far as I know, that is concerned with the Horace Club and its members all those years ago."

"There must be something else."

"It's probably in Latin," Katherine said, rolling her eyes.

"De lingua latina, libera nos, Domine?" Mr. Rush murmured with a sly smile.

"Oh no," Katherine said. "Not you too."

"Et tu, Brute?"

"Stop it, stop it."

And Katherine clapped her hands over her ears and

marched over to join Sister Mary Teresa and Mr. McFarland.

"I attended the fiftieth reunion of my class at Notre Dame," Benjamin Rush said to Kim. "It promised to be an attractive and nostalgic occasion."

"And was it?"

"We all said it was. We wandered around the campus with caps bearing the year of our graduation, we were feted and praised, indiscriminately. This is a not very subtle form of condescension. Unwitting condescension was the official attitude of our hosts. We were cute little old men to be humored."

"But you saw all your old friends?"

"I saw quite a few men in various stages of declension who bore the names of friends of my youth. They were impostors, of course."

Kim suspected that there was more to this seemingly inconsequential reminiscence, and of course there was.

"Reunions are dangerous events, Sister Kimberly. Extremely upsetting. I think we were all relieved to go home and get away from one another, and from a place that bore only slight resemblance to the school we attended."

"You're sorry you went?"

"Oh, I'd go again tomorrow. Reunions are also irresistible, once they are organized. Am I right in thinking that Sister Mary Teresa wants to bring back all the surviving girls of the Horace Club?"

"Invitations have already gone out."

"*Dii immortales!*"

"I had no idea you were such a Latinist, Mr. Rush."

"Nor did I. Suddenly it is coming back. We must have a language gland that secretes words and phrases if properly stimulated." Abruptly his hand went to his chin, and a blush suffused his parchment-skin face. Had she found the metaphor suggestive?

"Then I must apply for a transplant."

"I will add a codicil to my will." He was still blushing painfully. Nothing in her vows stood in the way of kissing this dear old man on the cheek, so she did, and he went away in confusion.

And so the die was cast. The McFarland gift was in the hands of John Handy, ready to be transferred to an account to be opened in the name of the Order of Martha and Mary Susan Dowd McFarland Center for the Classics. ("OMAMS-DMCFTC?" Joyce said. "That's some acronym.") The board consisted of Sisters Mary Teresa, president; Kimberly, vice-president; Joyce, secretary. Agnes DiLauria was hired to be the executive director of the center at a salary that made Joyce's eyes pop.

"My father never earned that kind of money."

"Inflation."

"Inflation? That's the Goodyear blimp."

It was, in fact, considerably less than Agnes had made as a self-employed counselor. For two years, since retiring, she had been living on social security alone, having neglected to set up a retirement plan during her working years.

As Kim had told Mr Rush, invitations had gone out to the last known addresses of members of the Horace Club, though not, needless to say, to Susan Dowd McFarland and Sonja Hansen. Margaret Mary was already here, of course, and Joanne Heit Mendoza was in Schaumburg, an hour away. How many of the other six would reply?

That afternoon, Sister Mary Teresa convened them in the dining room, a version of the meetings that were held when there were many members of the order and means had to be taken to insure that everyone knew everyone else. There was little reason for that in the house on Walton Street of course, but the coming of Margaret Mary had suggested to Emtee Dempsey that they might in a small way revive the custom.

"We used to call it our chapter of faults," Joyce remembered, though she was only a novice at the time.

"I have a whole book," Margaret Mary replied.

Emtee Dempsey took the occasion to explain the phrase "chapter of faults"—the get-together at which monks had publicly acknowledged their failings, and asked pardon from God and their brethren—and went on to apply the practice to themselves.

"*Mutatis mutandis*, of course, Margaret Mary."

Emtee Dempsey said a few things about what had attracted her to the order years ago, and it seemed to have been as much her reading about the redoubtable Blessed Abigail Keineswegs than any then member of the order that had constituted the attraction.

"Of course it was the educational work of the order that drew me, and at the college level. Many nuns taught grade school and found it fulfilling. I doubt that I could have."

"Of course you were meant to be a scholar."

"Meant to be," the old nun repeated. "It was a time of life when I could have been directed along any number of paths. If you had asked me then, I would not have known what the intellectual life was."

It was a quite natural transition when Emtee Dempsey asked Margaret Mary to tell them about herself. Kim expected their postulant to speak about her days as a student of the college, but she didn't.

"My life ended with the death of my husband and child," she said, in a calm voice. "Since then it is as if I have begun all over again. Not that I could ever forget Paul or Emily." She stopped and took in a great mouthful of air. "I want my new life to be a way of remembering them."

She found that she was able, as she had not been before, to tell them the details of the accident that had taken her husband and daughter from her. Paul had built a playhouse for Emily in the yard, the kind every girl dreams of, her own little house. Before she furnished it, Paul wanted to finish the interior. He worked very late one night and the next morning he took her out to show her the results.

Again Margaret Mary took a deep breath. "There was a tremendous explosion. It shook the house, cupboards flew open, dishes and glasses were crashing to the floor. I had no idea what had happened. I ran into the yard, screaming for Paul. And I saw that the playhouse was no more. The explosion had taken place there."

The explanation was that he had left cans of paint and thinner there when he finished the night before. When he and Emily went inside it, his morning cigarette ignited the gases that had accumulated overnight, causing the explosion.

They sat in silence for a minute, then Emtee Dempsey began to talk, a soft-voiced, reflective homily about the way in which different lives interweave to become one religious community, that the joys and sorrows of each become those of all.

Margaret Mary's was a haunting story and Kim looked differently on her after that. She had seemed so self-assured and competent a person, a wonder in the computer room, not someone who had been touched by tragedy. Kim of course had known that she had lost her husband and family, but it had had no vivid meaning for her.

"That was very moving," Kim said to Emtee Dempsey, when she was in the study helping her with her letters.

"Yes."

"I feel so unscathed by life when I hear a story like that."

"Don't envy others their sorrows. You will have enough of your own."

Kim continued to file photocopies of the letters the old nun had written. When she turned she was surprised to see her seated inactive at her desk.

"Is something wrong?"

"I was reflecting on the similarities between Margaret

Mary's story and Mr. McFarland's account of Susan's death."

"How did she die?"

"An explosion. The engine of her car."

"Good heavens."

"He lacerates himself for it, of course. He had had labor disputes of a particularly vicious kind, and the suspicion is that he was the intended victim. It is still under investigation."

Richard's announcement that they had identified the serial killer not only dominated the news of the city, it was also the major topic of conversation on Walton Street. That the son of Richard's proposed literary collaborator should be the murderer stirred up speculation throughout the Chicago area.

Emtee Dempsey pleaded with him to come tell them all about it, but he was reluctant even to spend time on the telephone.

"We're getting calls from people who claim to know him. And they're localized. With any luck, it won't be long. I just hope he doesn't take off and is picked up in some other city. We've blanketed the area where most of the calls are coming from."

"Barrington?"

"No, Schaumburg."

And it was in Schaumberg that Oscar was taken into custody.

He was, he claimed, returning to his mother's house and his reaction to the arrest took much of the triumph out of it for Richard and his crew.

"I heard about my mom and I wanted to be here for her funeral."

This declaration was played again and again over television. The alleged Oscar looked boyish and incapable of the acts of which he was accused.

"That's typical," Richard said, dropping by at last. He had the look of a weary but victorious general.

Equally typical were the comments of neighbors who, from what they knew of him, could not imagine Eric doing these dreadful things. And to his mother as well? Impossible.

With success came criticism too, of course. Unnamed sources on Richard's team suggested that the case would have moved along a lot more quickly if the director had not become emotionally involved. There was the not-too-subtle suggestion that Richard had been romantically involved with Astrid Johansen. This was very bad.

"Lois had been counting on that book money," Richard explained to the sisters. "Like an idiot I told her we would be on Easy Street. Now this. The papers are saying the book deal fell through because Astrid and I argued. If I want argument I can get all I want at home. Just kidding."

Typical too were calls from men claiming to be the real Oscar.

The odd thing was that, with the presumed killer arrested, the fear had not gone away. It was as if, having come to see that dreadful things can happen to people you know, suburbanites no longer felt safe. When might it all start up again, with some other deranged young man working out his psychosis on defenseless women?

"Is he being cooperative, Richard?" Sister Mary Teresa asked.

Richard frowned. "My job is to find them and to provide sufficient evidence for a judge to hold them and the prosecutor to indict and try them. Now it's in the hands of the lawyers."

"Do you expect difficulty?"

"I always expect difficulty."

"You doubt this is the man?"

"Do I doubt it? No. I've questioned him, or tried to. He has an idiot named Beamer for a lawyer, the cousin of one of the witnesses. But no, I have no doubt. I looked him in the eye and saw the same cornered look as when he panicked and ran through the traffic on I-94. That run settles it for me."

"So the boy you've arrested and the boy you chased are the same."

"Absolutely," Richard said, but he looked at her warily.

"Have your technical specialists been of help to you?"

"There's no difficulty placing him in the house where his mother was killed. He lived there. You're asking what the judge is asking."

"Did you ask him about his mother?"

"He broke down and cried like a baby. It was the first time he showed any emotion. He sat there like a cigar store Indian, expressionless, until that question. It was as if he realized for the first time that he was going to have to answer for the horrible things he had done."

Kim could see that Richard was on pins and needles, urging on all the technicians and scientist who were going through the dust and prints and fragments brought back from the various sites and waiting for Judge Pence in Schaumburg to decide whether there was sufficient evidence to bind over Eric Johansen.

Before Richard's visit, Emtee Dempsey had been closeted with Margaret Mary in her study for a long time and when Kim came in afterward, there was no indication what it was about. The novice director fulfilling her duties? Kim asked a few leading questions that went nowhere, and it was clear the old nun didn't think it was something Kim had to know.

She was also shut out from the purpose of an even longer session with Katherine. Voices rose and at one point Katherine opened the door and it was clear she was extremely angry with her old friend, but the door closed with Katherine still on the other side and when she emerged a half hour later, she went to the door muttering to herself and was very distracted when Kim said good-bye. Katherine looked at her almost as if surprised she was there. Then she shook her head.

"The decay of a great mind."

And then she was gone.

When Judge Caroline Pence ruled that there was insufficient evidence to hold Eric Johansen, the public reaction was outrage. Television commentators and editorial writers had a field day with the practice of judges in making the work of the police impossible. It was so common as to seem commonplace for men everyone knew to be guilty to walk free because of a legal technicality or a narrow application of an admittedly important safeguard.

Interviewers were so palpably sympathetic that Richard was tempted to speak to more reporters than he did. He did not of course criticize the judge, the rules of evidence, or the legal system generally. His tack was that police investigation was one part of a very complicated process in which some citizens are tried by other citizens.

The less he said the more they loved it. He and his team were cast in the role of the good guys, Pence was the bad guy, and Eric Johansen returned to his mother's condo, a free man.

"Of course Pence is right," Richard said to Schwartz.

"I know."

What they needed was physical evidence that linked

Eric to one of the murders. All the eyewitnesses they had, including Richard, were engaged in begging the question. The killings themselves could be linked in a variety of ways—Mitzi Earl's scarf, the condition of the bodies. Eric had been identified as being in the area of two of the killings—that of Irma Walsh and of his mother.

"I thought Pence might take as sufficient my seeing him where I did right before his mother's body was found and the fact that he ran."

But she hadn't, so their job continued. Richard put Eric under overt surveillance; Pence had granted him that at least. Night and day, Eric was being watched and he knew he was being watched. It was this kind of psychological pressure that had led to the arrest of John Wayne Gacy, and Richard hoped it would work here. Like Gacy, Eric responded to the surveillance as if it were a game, and he wasted a lot of their time trying to elude those watching him.

The hundreds of prints that had been lifted from the various sites were compared with those they had taken of Eric when he was arrested, and Richard's optimism that it would be a matter of hours at most for a match to be made faded as not hours but days went by.

"He's the guy," Schwartz said, as if he could sense the worm of doubt in Richard's scowling reflections.

"He's got to be."

They went through it all, step by step, if only to retain their confidence that the man they had under twenty-four-hour surveillance was indeed Oscar.

Mitzi Earl had escaped the first attempt on her and had directed the identikit experts in constructing a portrait of the man who had tried to shove her into a car in front of the house on Walton Street. She hurtled over the gaping car door, leaving her assailant with the scarf she had been wearing.

A day later Mitzi was strangled in the Palmer House with that same scarf.

The man who had assaulted her and the man who killed her were the same man and that man was the one whose picture they had shown to the people working in the ice cream store in Barrington and gotten statements that they had seen the man pictured in their store on the night that Irma Walsh was last seen in the store next to theirs.

When Richard came face-to-face with Eric Johansen, he knew he was confronting the man in the picture Mitzi had helped them construct. Astrid Johansen, his mother, it would be learned when Joanne Mendoza discovered the body, had been killed about the time Richard saw Eric in the vicinity of the house.

And Eric had run like a scared rabbit.

The more he thought of it, the more Richard felt that the commentators and editorialists were right. It was circumstantial and inferential and lots of things, but it was a tight fit.

"He's the guy," Schwartz repeated, and Richard agreed.

Richard was in Schwartz's office when the call came in that a man in Schaumburg had called 911 to report an attack on his daughter.

His name was Mendoza.

Richard was on his feet immediately and on his way to his car and Schwartz came running after him.

Stella Mendoza had been taken to the hospital by the paramedics and it was there Richard had his first talk with Joanne. Or tried to. She sat, hunched over, her hair a mess, tears rolling steadily from her eyes. They had given her a blanket and she had it pulled around her shoulders, but even so every once in a while she would shiver in the warm emergency room. He already knew that she had arrived in time to save her daughter, driving the attacker off with a mother's rage. For the moment she had had the strength of ten, now she seemed only a tenth of her usual self.

"Did you get a good look at him?"

She just stared at him.

"Could you identify him?"

Her mouth opened several times, then closed. Her husband, standing beside her, clearly wanted Richard to leave her alone.

"Joanne, who did this?"

"Eric!" she shouted. "Eric!"

And her body shook convulsively as she sobbed. Richard was on his feet, looking an apology at Jorge Mendoza, and took Schwartz aside.

"I want her watched. If it takes a dozen people, I want her watched. We don't want another Mitzi Earl."

"But how could it be Eric?" Schwartz asked.

Richard took his arm and began to squeeze. "And I don't want anyone who was supposed to be keeping Eric under surveillance providing security for this woman!"

"I'm going over there right now."

"No. *We're* going over there."

They rode in silence to the Johansen house. This was a terrible way to get the link they needed but now they had a surviving victim to identify Eric Johansen as her assailant. Pence wouldn't hesitate now.

"They're going to think we deliberately let him slip away."

"I know that."

"They're going to say that at the Johansen house we risked another killing in order to get the clincher we needed."

"Schwartz, you'd better talk to these guys. All right?"

"I'm as mad as you are."

"No you're not."

On duty at the Johansen house, still unaware of the attack on Joanne, were three officers, in contact by walkie-talkie, triangulating the house. Schwartz slipped into the passenger seat of an unmarked car manned by a cop named Broestl, who had a graying crew cut.

"He in there?"

"He's in there."

"Sure?"

"He hasn't shown himself all afternoon, but he's in there."

"Check with the others."

Broestl called the other two officers, Hayden and Chilton, and they said the same thing. They hadn't seen him all afternoon but he was in there.

Schwartz took the walkie-talkie.

"This is Schwartz. Can you all hear me?"

They could hear him.

"The man you haven't seen all afternoon attacked a woman less than an hour ago."

Broestl got out of the car and headed for the house with his weapon drawn and Richard, as he followed Broestl and Schwartz, saw Hayden and Chilton converging on the house from the back.

Broestl pulled open the storm door and beat on the inner door with his fist, as if he meant to break it down. While he was pounding on the door, he was leaning on the bell.

"He's in there," he muttered. "He's in there."

There was the sound of a lock being turned. Broestl stepped back. The door opened and Eric Johansen looked out at them, a quizzical smile on his face.

27

Few could have been happier than Katherine Senski when Richard and his cohorts first arrested the man they had been seeking, the man who had terrorized the lives of so many and who had struck close to those dear to Katherine, first assaulting, later strangling, a young woman whom Katherine had come to admire. It gave Katherine a sense that life had not become entirely meaningless and absurd, and that some crimes are indeed punished.

"It is over," she said to Sister Mary Teresa over the phone.

"Nearly over, perhaps."

"You mean the trial?"

"If he is indeed brought to trial. I have been talking with Benjamin Rush and he shares my belief that a judge may very well let him go."

"Bosh."

But this had happened. Katherine could not face her old friend when the outrageous decision of Judge Pence became known. But she was asked to come to the house and go she did, prepared to weather Emtee Dempsey's reminder that she had after all expressed the thought that this would indeed happen. But her old friend did nothing of the kind.

"There is something I need done and only you can do it, Katherine."

This disarmed her, of course, prepared as she was for a touch of smugness, an air of I-told-you-so. *Sed tantum dic verbo.*

Emtee Dempsey laughed. "By the time the Center opens, Latin will have become the language of this house."

"Just say the word."

Katherine's restored spirits soon fled when she heard what Emtee Dempsey had in mind.

"I have read again Astrid Johansen's fascinating book on the Kensington Rune stone. I regret that I did not get to talk with her about it before . . . " She tossed up her hands.

The book was dedicated to Lars. Emtee Dempsey assumed this was her estranged husband. Emtee Dempsey had checked and no Lars Johansen had inquired with either the Schaumburg police or the funeral home concerning Astrid.

"I might suggest to Richard that he make official police inquiries in Austin, Minnesota, but I have ruled that out. Still, such an inquiry requires professional connections, and what connections rival those of the police if not the freemasonry of journalists?"

"You want a Lars Johansen of Austin, Minnesota, notified that his former wife Astrid has been murdered in Illinois?"

Emtee Dempsey winced. "It might be better to omit the manner of her death and mention the date of the funeral."

"Wouldn't it be a good deal easier to ask her son?"

"Of course it would. Margaret Mary made a special trip to Schaumburg to ask him."

"And?"

"He says he has no father."

"Well, then."

"It is a biological impossibility for him not to have a father."

"What he must mean is that he doesn't know him."

"He may mean that, yes. I am dissatisfied. I am very anxious to learn if such a man exists. I am confident that he does, and that he came to Illinois."

"Why are you so interested in the former husband of a woman whose son murdered her after unspeakable acts?"

"Katherine, it is essential that he *not* know of my interest nor of that of anyone else connected with the Order of Martha and Mary."

"Oh, no! Please don't tell me you are spinning wild theories about these murders being connected with the order."

"There is no doubt that they are."

"I am going. I will not sit here and listen to someone I admire as much as I do you talk arrant nonsense." Katherine rose, went to the door and opened it as she said this, her voice thundering as she did.

"Please sit down, Katherine. Have you ever doubted me in the past?"

"Of course."

"I mean on the basis you now do. I know the meaning of the look that comes now and again into your eye and Benjamin Rush's. You think I am going gaga. You have thought so before."

"That's true."

"And you were wrong."

So there was to be an I-told-you-so after all. Katherine could nor deny that on at least one previous occasion she had been certain that the old nun was no longer playing with a full deck.

"If you expect me to conclude that therefore I must be wrong now, well, you are a better logician than that."

"Humor me, Katherine."

"That is precisely what I would be doing."

"That is all I ask, then."

Katherine could have refused. She could have explained that a true friend does not aid and abet a friend in her folly. She could have let the friendship of almost half a century cool and wither. So she agreed to enlist journalistic colleagues in Austin, Minnesota, in conveying to Lars Johansen—first having ascertained that he was the man indeed sought—that his former wife had been killed in Illinois and that a question had arisen as to the heir of her considerable property.

"You have a low opinion of him, don't you?"

"It would be unwise to assume he harbors an affection for his former wife that would bring him all the way from Austin to Schaumburg." She made it sound like the Lewis and Clark Expedition. "It is safer to assume that he has an acquisitive sense."

"Sister, I do this only because your name will not be brought in."

"That is a condition!"

An hour later Katherine was chatting with Ginger about the events in Schaumburg and casually mentioned that Astrid must have had a husband.

"That's right. She has that dreadful son."

"I wonder if he's heard."

"Is he still alive?"

"The marriage ended in divorce. I don't recall any description of her as a widow."

"Maybe he wouldn't want to be told of her death. Divorces can sometimes be awful."

"She dedicated one of her books to Lars. If that's her husband, he could still be found where she wrote the book. She indicates in the preface that she was a native of Austin."

"Texas?"

"Minnesota."

"I didn't know there was an Austin, Minnesota."

"It is where Spam was originated. Leslie Caron married the scion of the Hormel family. It is where Cecilia Vespertina got her start. There must be a newspaper there. Why don't you look it up?"

Ginger found the paper listed in the Bowker reference book, and Katherine said it would be interesting to put a call through and see if there was a Lars there. Ginger needed little prompting now. Katherine shook a cigarette free from the package on Ginger's desk and lit it.

With her hand over the receiver, Ginger said, "This could make a great column."

Listening to Ginger's half of the conversation, Katherine reflected how instantaneous everything had become. Even as Ginger spoke, a message from Austin began to emerge from her fax machine. It was a photocopy of a page from the Austin telephone directory containing the addresses and phone numbers of eleven Johansens, Lars. Obviously it would have been unrealistic to expect a reporter from the Austin paper to check out the eleven in search of the one they wanted.

"What now?" Ginger said.

"I'll take this to my office and start calling."

"I wish we'd gotten better results, Katherine."

"This is more than I deserve."

"You forgot your cigarette."

"No I didn't."

The first two numbers she called were blanks: Not only was it not the Lars Johansen who had once been married to Astrid, they had no idea who that Lars Johansen might be. The third number was answered by a woman, which posed a problem. If this was the present Mrs. Johansen, she was unlikely to be eager to be reminded of a predecessor.

"Is Lars there?"

"Who's calling?"

"This is long distance in Illinois."

"Oh God, what's happened?"

Katherine thought about that question. "He hasn't been around?"

"Not for weeks. What is it?"

And then, just for Emtee Dempsey, giving her the benefit of the doubt, Katherine asked, "Where in Illinois do you think he is?"

"I thought you said you were calling from Illinois."

"That's right. The Illinois Lottery has to verify all out-of-state purchasers before making payment."

"Did Lars win?"

"It's not that simple. A woman won, Astrid Johansen."

"But he was married to her."

"Do you suppose he came here?"

"I told you I haven't heard from him for weeks. But Astrid was his wife. How much did she win?"

"We're not allowed to give out that information on the telephone. Is there any chance he'll be getting in touch with you?"

"I don't know. Maybe."

"Please write down this number."

Katherine gave the telephone number at her apartment. Afterward, she sat very still, wondering what it was she had learned.

After several minutes, she called Walton Street and told Emtee Dempsey what she had done in fulfillment of her request. She gave her the telephone conversation verbatim.

"Is that what you wanted to know?"

"It's exactly what I wanted to know. What a rascal you are, Katherine. The Illinois Lottery! What wild hopes you have raised."

"I figure you have as much chance of showing what you want to show as I have of winning the lottery."

"Katherine, people win the lottery every day."

"What does this tell you?"

"That the brother of Sonja Hansen has been in the vicinity for several weeks."

28

The guards who had been on duty watching Eric when Joanne Mendoza's daughter was saved by the appearance of her mother, suddenly possessed with the strength of ten in defense of her daughter's honor, all insisted that Eric could not have gotten out of the house.

"Not on my watch," Broestl said emphatically, and the others were equally certain.

"You mean he got out before you came on duty?"

"I mean no one left that house while I was on duty."

"Well, the man you say was in the house was more than a mile away, attempting to add another young woman to his list of victims."

The other members of the surveillance team were called in, everyone insisted that there was no way in the world Eric Johansen could have left that house without their knowing it. It was Eric's practice to go out and about during the day, seemingly just to test the skills of his guardians, but all of these excursions were duly accounted for and Eric had been checked out of the house, followed while he was away, and checked back into the house when he returned. The team was adamant that no unobserved absence from the house was possible.

"Unless he's got a secret way out," Broestl said.

The first time this was mentioned, Richard let it go by as simply a way of underscoring that Eric could not have gotten out, but the second time he responded.

"If you all are as certain as your are, that begins to look like the only reasonable explanation."

"There has to be a reasonable explanation."

"He can't be in two places at the same time."

"There must be a secret way out."

"I say, let's go in there and tear the place apart until we find a tunnel or whatever it is."

"The thing of it is, unless we do that, we don't *know* he's in there right now."

It was an unnerving thought that Eric might even now be molesting some other young woman. Remembering poor Mitzi Earl, Richard called the Mendoza residence and asked about Stella.

"She's as well as can be expected," Jorge said. "When are you going to put that maniac behind bars?"

"You're certain Stella is there."

"Of course she's here."

"Would you look?"

It took several minutes before the irate Mendoza agreed to go look. He put down the phone with an unnecessary bang, and Richard stood listening to the muted sound of the Mendoza household until Jorge returned.

"The place is surrounded by cops, my wife hasn't left her side since it happened, hell yes, she's here."

So Richard went before Judge Pence seeking a warrant enabling them legally to enter the Johansen house and look for a secret exit. Caroline Pence had a narrow face made narrower by huge spectacles, in the lenses of which her eyes appeared like children at a window. She had ascended the bench three years out of law school; she was regularly spoken of for higher things; whatever she did she did for the record, on the expectation that the day would come when her judicial actions to date would be gone over by hostile as well as by friendly critics.

"You've got to be kidding."

They were in Pence's chambers where, without her robe, wearing jeans and a Dartmouth sweatshirt, she looked scarcely older than Stella Mendoza.

"I am dead serious. As Stella Mendoza might very well have been dead. Eric Johansen assaulted her; he can be identified by both the daughter and the mother who saved the situation. We thought he was in his house at the time. Obviously he couldn't have been there and attacking the Mendoza girl at the same time."

"That's true."

"Therefore, if he was at the Mendoza's, he could not have been at home at the same time."

"That's valid."

"But none of the 'expert' police officers keeping his house under surveillance saw him leave. Therefore he must be able to leave in a manner that is unobserved by those police officers."

Pence tapped on the frame of her glasses with a ball-point pen as she thought about. Then she had it.

"The answer is simple."

"What is it?"

"Those two women, in the excitement of the moment, thought they saw Eric Johansen, but of course they couldn't have."

"But they did!"

"How could they see in their house a man who was certifiably in his own house miles away?"

"With two eyewitnesses he was certifiably in the Mendoza house."

"And three officers who swear he was in his own house. Lieutenant Moriarity, I needn't tell you that during these awful months women have been seeing Oscar under their beds at the same time and in different places all over the western suburbs."

Judge Pence smiled up at him in the smuggest way and it was difficult not to tell her he hoped Eric would come calling on *her* soon so that they might have this same discussion again.

"This is not just a problem in logic, your honor."

"Then you're admitting that your request suffers from a logical problem?"

The constabulary is the arm of the law, the instrument of its observance and the maintenance of the peace within which alone that observance can be assured. The police fit into a triangle whose other two points are the legislature and the judiciary. There should be understanding and sympathy between the three. It was Richard's belief that Judge Pence was invoking law to prevent him from enforcing the law and bringing to trial a man only an idiot, or a judge who had risen too quickly to the bench, could think was not guilty as sin. . . .

"The answer's no," Richard informed Schwartz afterwards.

"No?"

"She thinks the Mendozas mistakenly identified a copy-cat Oscar as Eric Johansen."

"Maybe we should start making obscene phone calls to her chambers."

"She would want to discuss the exact meaning of the proposition."

They doubled the size of the surveillance team and had six rather than three officers on watch at all times. It grew on them that there was a tunnel that led from the house to some point far away from which Eric could emerge and do whatever he wished unobserved by them. Or it might lead to another house.

"I'm going to talk to the people who developed these condos," Schwartz said.

Why not? The only thing left to them was pointless routine until Eric succeeded in another attack and they could pin it on him.

Depressed and angry, reluctant to go home and visit his frustration on Lois, Richard was almost relieved to find a message asking him to stop by the house on Walton Street. He was surprised to find the place bursting at the seams; all the inhabitants of the house were there, plus Agnes Di-Lauria, Benjamin Rush, and Katherine Senski, who had brought along her colleague Ginger Federstein.

"Hail the conquering hero," the old nun cried, without irony, and the others looked at him with an admiration he had not seen since he gave the lecture in Schaumburg weeks before.

He held up his hand. "This is a little premature. The judge put the kibosh on the search warrant."

"Tell us, tell us."

Emtee Dempsey followed his account of the conversation with the judge with great interest, asking him to repeat the exchange with her.

"Where did she go to school?"

"Law school?"

"College."

Sister Mary Teresa expressed surprise, even disappointment, that Judge Pence was not a graduate of the College of Martha and Mary. This was not the kind of sympathy Richard needed.

"She is essentially right, Richard. Of course there is no secret tunnel through which the boy leaves the house."

"How do you know that?"

"Judge Pence has the right idea. The man who tried unsuccessfully to attack dear Joanne's daughter is not the man your colleagues can verify was in the house being watched at the time of the incident."

"Sister, both Joanne and her daughter agree that the

man is the man in the picture we have been circulating."

"The one Mitzi Earl helped you with?"

"Yes."

"And it is a picture of the man who attacked her as well. The answer would seem to be that it is not a picture of the man you have under surveillance."

This was worse, far worse, than Judge Pence, but of course Richard had had previous experience with the annoying omniscience of the old nun. Here she sat in this comfortable house, writing away on a history of the Middle Ages, not really wired into the times in which she lived, never going much farther away than the cathedral when they didn't have a priest to say Mass for them in their chapel, and she was confidently explaining events that had occurred miles away as if she were an eyewitness, or better than an eyewitness.

"Oscar is not Eric?"

"That seems obvious."

"Any idea who he might be?."

She turned her great headdress to one side and regarded him askance. "You're testing me."

Richard managed to hide his anger. "Now you're going to tell me that Oscar, who isn't Eric, is the man who killed all those women and attacked Stella Mendoza? Sister Mary Teresa, I looked him in the eye and the man who looked back at me is Oscar. And that man was Eric Johansen."

The old nun wagged her finger at him playfully. "You won't catch me that easily. I remember your comment at the time."

The others were following this exchange with keen attention. They too seemed to see him in the role of one testing the old nun's sharpness. "What comment?"

"That he seemed younger than Mitzi had made him look in the picture."

That had been his impression when he turned and looked the man in the eye: He was Oscar but a younger

Oscar than the picture they were distributing. But the construction of such pictures, while an art, is not a science. The difference in ages need not have meant anything, and indeed he had forgotten it.

"You remembered that, did you?"

"I also noticed you were careful not to allude to it again. How could I not find that significant? The obvious explanation was that you were simply playing your cards close to the vest. That is the phrase, isn't it? When I did see the significance of your remark, I wanted to salute you, but I held my tongue. I know that you do not like others interfering in your work. It spurred me on a course which led me to the conclusion you too will have reached. Surely, there is no longer reason for secrecy? Or are you just teasing me, to see if we have indeed reached the same conclusion."

"Go ahead and say it."

"Oscar is Lars Johansen, of course. The boy's father."

After a moment's stunned silence, the room erupted into applause, and excited talk. Richard was aware of Kim looking at him. Her expression was not exactly accusing, but it was obvious that she understood perfectly how Sister Mary Teresa had made him party to her conclusion.

Or hypothesis. He went into the kitchen and got on the phone, directing a full-tilt search for Lars Johansen, the estranged husband of Astrid and the father of Eric.

"Would he have a record?"

"Let's find out."

He called Judge Pence and told her of this new line of inquiry.

"That is compatible with what I suggested during our talk, isn't it?"

"It was pretty clear you didn't like the idea of bilocation."

She laughed a girlish laugh. "For myself, I'd love it."

"One Judge Pence is enough."

"I'll take that as a compliment."

"Thank you for your help, your honor. Our last conversation opened up the new path of inquiry."

Had Emtee Dempsey felt as phony as this when she attributed to him her guess about Lars Johansen?

It became clear that she had done a lot more than simply imagine the alternative Oscar. Katherine had Ginger tell him of her inquiries in Austin and then she told him of her Illinois Lottery ploy that had elicited the information that Lars was in the Chicago area. Richard went back to the phone.

29

During the exchange between Richard and Sister Mary Teresa, two things were clear to Kim. First, that much had been going on in the house of which she had been kept unaware, and, second, that Richard had not come to the conclusion for which Emtee Dempsey gave him credit. The achievement was all hers. Kim didn't know whether she was more ashamed of the old nun for manipulating Richard or of Richard for allowing it to happen. She would speak to both of them about it later.

Katherine Senski was banging her hand on the coffee table as Richard returned from the kitchen.

"Enough of this adulation," she said in her loud, husky voice. "I am going to put our good friend and hostess on the spot." She turned to Sister Mary Teresa. "In past weeks, you have been distressing me, and others, by making the absurd suggestion that these terrible murders would somehow be shown to be connected with the Order of Martha and Mary. Very well, Sister, will you now publicly admit that there is no such connection? You and Richard Moriarity can bask in your triumph, but what on earth has Lars Johansen got to do with the M&M's?"

She fell back in her chair, glaring benevolently at the

old nun, awaiting her admission. Benjamin Rush, seemingly dismayed by what Katherine had said, began to speak but the old nun asked him to wait.

"You are being willfully obtuse, Katherine. Would you admit that?"

"I will not."

"But you were so helpful in tracking down Lars Johansen. I assumed you knew what his importance was."

"If he is the murderer of these young women, that is important enough. Where is his connection with the order?"

Sister Mary Teresa stared at Katherine, as if dumbfounded, and the silence grew. Benjamin Rush closed his eyes, and his lips moved in what might have been prayer. And then the old nun spoke.

"Lars Johansen is the brother of Sonja Hansen."

Katherine's mouth dropped open. Benjamin Rush's eyes widened and he looked at the old nun, startled, and then slowly a smile formed on his face.

"Margaret Mary, perhaps you should carry on from this point."

"No, no, Sister. You do it."

"It all comes back to the Horace Club, of course."

Sonja Hansen—the college records showed that she had changed her name to this shorter form—had been a brilliant student from Austin, Minnesota, who had done well in everything but excelled in the classics. If she had any fault it was that she took undue pride in her achievements and was not above embarrassing her teachers when they were guilty of some lapse of information.

"I think of the young Abelard, come to Laon to study and soon quarreling with his masters and eventually declaring himself a rival master and stealing away their students."

The Horace Club had been Sonja's idea, an assembly of classics majors who would in effect come under her tutelage. The college insisted that there must be a faculty moderator. Sister Mary Benedict was appointed.

"That was my name in religion," Agnes DiLauria said. "I was one of Sonja's teachers and I felt the sting of her arrogance more than once. I tried to prevent the formation of the club because I could see what Sonja was up to. Failing that, I agreed to be moderator."

Then came the famous matter of Ode 38 of Book One. The *Persicos odi, puer.* It had been a group project of the newly formed club and the effort extended over many months. Everyone contributed, and it was genuinely a common achievement, although Sonja of course was the guiding spirit. And it was a project that was kept secret from the moderator, who only knew about the club's more public activities.

The club had been formed when the girls were sophomores. In the second semester of junior year, Susan Dowd had come upon a translation of the Horatian ode in *Poetry.* The author was given as Sonja Hansen. Susan did not show the others in the club the issue but took it to Sister Mary Benedict.

"I can confess now that I seized upon this as a way of teaching Sonja a lesson she would not forget," said Agnes DiLauria. "I turned the matter over to the dean, and a committee was formed to make inquiry. We interviewed all the girls, keeping Sonja until last. Her disdain for the committee was palpable, her remarks about the other members of the club were contemptuous, and she was particularly insulting to me. When we met a last time to decide on a punishment, I proposed expulsion."

The girl was expelled, a proud young woman publicly humiliated. She returned home and the impossibility of explaining why she was there sent her into a despondency that ended with her taking her own life. Her brother Lars was her confidant. He vowed to avenge her.

"And that," Emtee Dempsey said, "is the connection between events at our college and this chain of brutal murders."

Margaret Mary was called on again, and she summarized the results of her research. All of the slain women, Liz Webster, Irma Walsh, and Amy Kuharic, though not of course Mitzi Earl and Astrid Johansen, were connected in some way to the Horace Club. The number who had died violent deaths was extraordinary.

"Richard and his team, you may be sure, will be tying this together more tightly for purposes of a trial."

"First we have to arrest him," Richard said. "The man is still at large."

"Margaret Mary warned the surviving members when she invited them to our coming reunion. But it would seem that only those in the Chicago area are in real danger."

That meant Margaret Mary, Joanne Mendoza, and most likely Agnes DiLauria. Agnes had been asked to stay in the house until the killer was apprehended and Joanne and her family were being well guarded because of the fear of a second attempt.

The following day, Katherine Senski received a telephone call. A man's voice asked if this was the woman who had called about the Illinois Lottery.

"I am with the *Chicago Tribune*."

"I was given this number and told to call."

Katherine felt a shiver of fear pass through her when she realized who was on the line. She developed the story she had told to the woman in Austin about Astrid Johansen's winning lottery ticket.

"I don't have the ticket."

"Oh we have the ticket." It was difficult to cross her fingers because of her rings. "Have you heard what has happened to her?"

"Yes."

"The ticket was one of the items in her purse."

"No kidding."

"Let me be clear, now. Our understanding is that you are her husband."

"We were married in April of 1964."

"Good. Now here is what you must do."

Katherine gave him careful instructions to come to her office at the *Tribune*. She assured him that it was simply a matter of turning the ticket over to him, as the *Tribune* had offered to act on the matter. Lars Johansen said he would be there within two hours.

Richard Moriarity was not in his office when she called, and Katherine demanded to know where he was.

"This is a matter of life and death."

"Yeah?"

It was infuriating that this claim, literally true, had lost its power from overuse.

"This is Katherine Senski of the *Chicago Tribune*. I insist on being put through to Lieutenant Moriarity."

"He is not giving out interviews."

There are moments when profanity, even if not weakened by overuse, is inadequate to the situation. But only God knows what Katherine might have said if a light on her phone had not indicated someone was trying to reach her. She cut off the insolent voice from Richard's office. Her caller was Sister Kimberly.

"Sister Mary Teresa wants to talk to you."

"Not as much as I want to talk to her. I have been trying to get through to your brother."

"He is here."

"God is good."

30

Richard took Katherine's call, listened, standing up as he did, then handed the phone to Emtee Dempsey and went down the hallway on the run. Now Kim watched the old nun listen, nodding, giving no indication about what was going on. Katherine's voice had been urgent and Kim regretted not getting some idea what it was all about before passing the call on to Richard.

"What is it?" she asked silently, forming the words with exaggerated care, so Emtee Dempsey could read her lips. The clear blue eyes regarded her through the round gold-rimmed lenses.

"Richard is on his way." Emtee Dempsey said into the phone. "Sister Kimberly will be along shortly."

She put down the phone and gave Kim instructions.

"What do you expect me to do there?"

"Witness what happens. I want an accurate report."

For heaven's sake. Kim went, reluctantly. That Katherine would expose herself to such danger in order to catch the man who had murdered all those people filled Kim with admiration, and with a sense of shame that she would not have such courage herself.

She parked the Volkswagen along the curb, in an opening too small for an ordinary-sized car, and got out. The wind off the lake combined with that roaring along the Chicago River, and she felt that she was being blown toward the door of the Tribune Building.

Inside, she hurried across the lobby toward an elevator whose door was just closing. She slipped in, the doors closed and she turned, sighing with relief, to face Oscar.

"What are you staring at?" he demanded.

"Nothing. I'm sorry." She turned away. The walls of the car seemed to be moving toward her, about to crush her. She was imprisoned with a serial killer. Floor 12 was illumined on the panel. Kim pushed 3. She had to get off.

"We passed three," he said behind her.

She punched 5 and 6 and 7 and then his hand closed over her wrist. He forced her to face him.

"What's wrong with you, lady?"

She felt an absurd impulse to cry out, "I'm no lady, I'm a nun." His eyes seemed at once vacant and full of menace and the sound of his breathing might have been that of a dragon from the most scary fairy tale of her childhood.

"You're hurting my wrist."

He let it go. "You punch buttons like that when this thing is in motion, you might jam it and we'll end up stuck between floors."

"I'm sorry."

She turned away. Was the elevator even moving? She had no sensation of movement, no sense that they were rising. But then with a little lurch they arrived at 12 and the doors slid open. He waited for her and she stepped out of the car.

"Kim!" It was Richard, surprised, annoyed. And then he saw the man emerge.

Gleason pushed Kim aside as he charged at the man whom Richard had since rushed and slammed to the floor of the elevator car. The door was trying to close, but the legs extending from it prevented that. Katherine and Ginger came to the door of an office and were directed to go back inside. An alarm bell began to sound, the elevator protesting its inability to close its door. And then Richard and Gleason, having manacled the man, got him to his feet and pushed him out of the elevator.

"Lars Johansen, I presume," Katherine said, sailing into the hall.

The elevator doors slid shut.

"Don't let that elevator get away," Richard barked and Gleason began to punch the down button.

"I just came for a lottery ticket," the battered captive said plaintively.

"You lost," Richard growled.

nder insistent instructions from Sister Mary Teresa and Katherine, Richard acknowledged the help of unspecified concerned citizens in the apprehension of Oscar, the serial killer who was now identified as Lars Johansen. Eric told a heartrending story of what life had been like before his mother had decided to move from Minnesota to Illinois.

"Did she say why Illinois?"

All he knew was that it had something to do with his father. Astrid's notebook that Richard had confiscated as a memento of their supposed collaboration was more informative. When Astrid began to publish, Lars resented it and spoke of the thwarted talent of his sister Sonja. This became an obsession with him, making it impossible for Astrid to remain with him. When the murders began in the western suburbs, her first thought had been fear of what Lars might do if he found her and Eric. Only gradually did she wonder if there was some possible connection with the tragic Sonja. The attack on Mitzi had brought to Astrid's attention that the order of nuns with whom Sonja had studied still existed. Richard's connection with the house on Walton Street had increased her apprehension. The proposal that they collaborate on a book that would tell the story of the investigation under way had been sincere, but it was also the means by which she hoped to keep informed of developments. After Mitzi was killed, Astrid became certain that her own life and Eric's were in danger. After all, she might discern what lay behind the apparently random killings.

"It's why Eric bolted when I confronted him. I startled him and his first impulse was to run."

"If only she had come to me," Emtee Dempsey said. Richard let it go.

Lars Johansen, after a day of surly silence, had decided to boast of his crimes. There was talk of a book and Richard winced when he heard of the writer who had been given permission to visit the accused.

Richard himself had been made into a hero of law enforcement by the media. Members of the team spoke of their leader in awed tones, expressing their amazement at the combination of scientific procedure and good old-fashioned hunches that had enabled him to find Oscar. The more Richard tried to downplay this interpretation, the more entrenched it became.

That changed when Ginger's column appeared in which she drew attention to the indispensable contributions of Sister Mary Teresa and Katherine Senski.

"You should have let me mention that," Richard groused.

"Please don't imagine that I gave Ginger permission, Richard. I am appalled."

"Do you know what they'll call me for hogging all the credit?"

"Sticks and stones, Richard. Sticks and stones."

Monsignor McCarthy said a Mass for all the victims of Lars Johansen to which Joanne and her daughter Stella came. It was in the dining room afterward that Katherine asked what the relationship of Irma Walsh to the Order of Martha and Mary had been. The old nun turned to Agnes DiLauria.

"She was my greatniece. My brother's granddaughter. I never dreamed . . . "

But it had apparently been the mention of Angelo Di-Lauria in the obituary that had first stirred Emtee Dempsey to see a relation of these murders to the order.

"Amy Kuharic was a puzzle until Margaret Mary produced her list of the members of the Horace Club coordinated with alumae records of marriages."

"I shall never doubt you again," Katherine Senski said fervently.

"Oh, I doubt that, my dear."

The formal opening of the Center was set for the turn of the year, but in the meantime, Agnes would be preparing for the great day.

"To think that none of this would have happened if Sonja had not been accused of plagiarism."

"No one could have foreseen the consequences."

"But a false accusation!" Agnes cried, genuine anguish in her voice.

"Why do you say that?"

"She did not intend to take credit for the other girls' work. I'm sure she was surprised when the translation appeared under her name alone. It wasn't a matter of plagiarism at all."

"There I must differ with you, Agnes." the old nun said.

She sent Kim to the study for the issue of *Poetry* in which the translation had appeared. "And bring the book on my desk as well, would you please, Sister?"

Armed with these materials, Sister Mary Teresa traced her finger down the page and then began to read:

> *I detest all luxury Oriental:*
> *bring me no fat leis of frangipani,*
> *boy, and don't search every forgotten nook where*
> *   lingers a late rose.*

Nothing but one plain little crown of myrtle
need you weave me. Myrtle is no disgrace to
you as page-boy, nor to your master, drinking,
shaded by vine-leaves.

"Isn't that beautiful?" She sighed. "I thought it had a familiar ring. And no wonder. Listen."

She opened the book Kim had brought and soon was reading the identical lines.

"What is that book?" Agnes asked.

"Gilbert Highet's *Poets in a Landscape*.[1] A wonderfully satisfying book."

Agnes was comparing the lines in *Poetry* with those in Highet.

"They are identical."

"Plagiarized," the old nun said. "I do not say that justice was done, Agnes. Nor injustice either."

"Well, I am glad to hear that," Benjamin Rush said.

"That justice was done or that injustice was not done?"

"They come to the same thing, don't they?"

"Oh, not at all, Benjamin," the old nun said. "Not at all."

---

[1]Alfred A. Knopf, New York, 1957, p. 145.